MW00906343

Came Home from the Grave

A Caleb Cove Mystery- Book 4

By Mahrie G. Reid

http://www.mahriegreid.com/

Copyright 2017 Mahrie E. Glab

ISBN 978-0-9937022-9-7

Jak-Win Books

Cover Design: Lorraine Paton

Copy Editor: Ted Williams

Thanks to my writing/publishing team of Diana Cranstoun, Sue Bergman and Swati Chavda, all talented authors in their own right. Also, thanks to Lorraine Paton for the cover art and Ted Williams for the copy editing. Once again you have all help bring my story to the page.

CHAPTER ONE

Constable Natalie Parker pulled her car into the detachment parking lot. Her pulse raced and the thump-thump echoed in her ears. Her stomach roiled. Whether with excitement or fear she wasn't sure. *Perhaps a bit of both.*

Her phone played the first beats of 'On the Road Again' and Constable Harvey Conrad's number showed in the display. *Harvey.* Her partner in hunting drug runners and tracking down a murderer or two. And he'd stood by her through her injury and time off. She grinned as she pushed the answer button. Recently they'd become more than friends.

"How'd it go, Sweetie?"

"Got it," she said.

"Excellent."

"Possibly."

"What do you mean?"

"I'm good at digging through data and tracking down information." She bit her lower lip. "You know. A two-sided coin. Wanting to be in the field and needing to be safe."

"We went through this. You're as good in the field as in the office." He paused. "Nat," he said, using the name only he used for her, "it's time to get back on the horse. Even if you decide later to make changes, you need to go back for your own peace of mind."

Natalie pinched the bridge of her nose and counted to six. "Darn you, Conrad. You sound like the head-doc."

"We're two smart people," Harvey said. "Believe us."

"I know. Just momentary cold feet," she agreed. A shiver

rippled through her. "The explosion still haunts me at times."

"You'll be fine. Now, m'girl, go get-em'."

She laughed. Harvey always stabilized her. "Get to work yourself, Conrad." She signed off and headed for her unit.

In the second-floor hall of the squat, brick building she squared her shoulders, ran a hand through her too-short hair and reached for the office door handle. Inside she nodded to her team members. They knew she hoped to return to active duty and, even though they'd appreciated the extra help she'd given with paperwork, they understood. She took the form and waved it, giving a thumbs up.

"Way to go." One voice rose over the others.

Another co-worker gave her the okay sign. "Glad you're ready to hit the pavement."

Superintendent Brayburn loomed in his office door. "All right you crew, back to work. Crimes to solve and paper work to handle." He gave her a curt nod. "Sounds like you're ready for active duty, Parker." He ushered her into his office, closed the door, and took his seat. "We've appreciated your work in the office, but we can use you back in the field."

"Thanks." What else could she say?

"You were blown up," he said. "Are you sure you're ready?"

Way to be blunt, boss. She nodded. "My psych evaluation agrees as does the neurological report. Maybe it is a case of what doesn't kill me makes me stronger." She didn't mention the reluctance of both doctors about the lurking potential for migraines.

Brayburn continued. "I'll be up front with you. I *am* concerned about sending you back in the field. Even the hardiest officers would be shaky after what you've been through."

"I'm…."

He held up a finger. "I know you think you're fine. And you may have convinced the docs you are. But know this," he said and pointed the finger at her. "If there is any sign a relapse would compromise a case, I'll pull you off any investigation so fast your head will spin."

No point in arguing. "Yes, sir."

He picked up his pen. "Go finish the files you've been working on this week. You'll be in the field when I decide." His phone rang, and he dismissed her with a wave.

Natalie stood, snapped a mock salute and went to her own desk. *Am I annoyed or relieved at the delay?* She planted both hands on her chair back. *Why do I even ask? Six weeks on desk duty. I am more than ready to get out of this office.* Taking her seat, she opened the one file left on her desk from the day before.

Moments later, Brayburn stood in his office door and summoned her again. She grimaced mentally, not daring to let it show on her face. *He never crooks his finger at the guys, only me.* One of the several habits that betrayed his old boy thinking. The subtle distinction bothered her now more than before the accident.

"Change of plans," he said. "We caught a new case." He raised his voice. "Sorry boys, but the lovely lady officer is not going to be available to help you. I need her elsewhere." *Yes, pretty boys, you're on your own. Like Brayburn would ever say such a thing.*

A collective groan sounded. At least *they* seemed to be sincere in appreciating her efforts.

She followed Brayburn into his office, her heart pounding. Did she want out of the office? Yes. Was she comfortable with the possibility? Maybe.

No door closing this time. He picked up a note. "We've had a call from a Constable Harvey Conrad in Bridgewater."

"Harvey?" she spoke without thought.

Brayburn looked up. "You know him?"

"Ah-HM. Quite well. We've worked together in Caleb's Cove from time to time." *And he helped me with a few other things during my recovery. But that is not your business.*

"Well, Caleb's Cove is at it again. A kid found, well, his dog found, what seems to be a human, skeletal arm and hand."

She clenched one hand. She knew almost everyone in Caleb's Cove. "Adam and Mutt."

Brayburn checked the note and nodded. He peered at her. "Are you okay?"

"A bit surprised," she said. "Adam is only twelve. It probably upset him." *Or he's loving the excitement.*

"Well, I need you down there again. The dog hauled the hand home. So, first, and Conrad has started on this, is to figure out where he found it. If you can find out where it came from, we can decide if an investigation is needed." He picked up his pen, his usual dismissal action.

He thinks it's nothing, so I get the call. She clamped her mouth over words threatening to spill out. *But anything that gets me out of this office and lets me spend time with Harvey is fine by me.* Natalie stood and marched out.

Leave it to Brayburn to hand her a straightforward case. One that would die a natural death if there were no more body parts. She grabbed her purse. Checked her gun and headed down the hall, dialing Harvey as she went.

"So, you drew the short straw?" His laugh punctuated his words. "Suits me fine."

"Looks like it. I think the boss figures it's an easy case for my first day back in the field."

"Right. As if anything out here is easy. The damn curse on the island always seems to rear its head."

"What? You're worried because there have been three murders, a serial killer and a kidnapping in the past six years?" She outlined the obvious, a running joke between them.

"You know the curse is the reason I stay," Harvey said. "With it, and the ever-present threat of drug runners, my life is exciting."

"Sure, Harvey, sure.

He laughed. "When will you be here?"

"In about three hours. I'll give you a heads up and meet you at the café. No, wait. Too public. How about over at the security office. I'll let Devon know we're coming and will probably use the cabin as well as the office."

"Works for me. See you."

Caleb's Cove. She loved it there, except when death permeated the air. The headache that never quite died, loomed behind her eyes. *Focus. Black pavement. Two squad cars. Three steps. Four trees.* The exercise steadied her brain. The ability to focus in the present came with long practice. The routine and a few minutes with her eyes closed pushed back the headache.

The sun warmed her head, but she shivered. No one she knew in Caleb's Cove deserved the secrets a corpse could dig up. But with secrets came answers. The answers were why she'd became a police officer.

Her father's words ran through her memory. *Policing is about justice for the victims, help for the weak, and order in the community.* Before he'd disappeared while undercover and been declared dead, she'd heard them often. *To be a good officer, you need to know yourself, be true to your core values and always do everything you can to help good triumph over evil."*

She turned the car onto Robie Street. Tension tightened the muscles between her shoulder blades and mixed excitement and fear twisted her stomach. In the past, secrets in Caleb's Cove had spiraled into murders. She shivered. If they found a murdered body, would it dig up old secrets?

CHAPTER TWO

Natalie slowed on the dirt road behind Crescent Beach. Sunbathers lounged on towels spread on white sand. Sun glinted off rolling waves and children chased each other, splashing along the water's edge. *Situation normal.* Across the bridge, she turned right and headed to the corner of Gerber's Lane and Westerly Road. Minutes later, she rolled down the lane with tree-shaded houses on the right and seagrasses stretching over the dunes on the left.

At the estate, she pulled up at the Caleb Cove Security Agency offices. She still marveled how her brother's friends, Greg Cunningham and Sam Logan, had built such a successful worldwide security business. Best part, the place had better equipment than her detachment, and she got to use the equipment whenever she liked.

Harvey's dark, cross–over vehicle squatted on the tarmac. Harvey himself leaned against the back wheel well, toothpick in his mouth, and Mutt lounging by his feet. She smiled at his habitual stance. He checked his watch and planting his feet flat, pushed away from the car until standing stable. Beside him, Mutt levered up his front end and hauled up his rear parts, until both man and dog stood watching her.

"You made good time," Harvey noted. "You didn't exceed the speed limits, did you? Hate to have to ticket you?" He laughed and hugged her.

"Me?" She jutted her chin. "Never."

"Welcome back," Harvey said. "Before we get started, I should warn you."

"What. About speeding?"

He shook his head. "I've had a call, the word is out and help is on its way."

Visions of previous cases offered an option. "Please don't tell me the whole of Caleb's Cove has found out and is joining us."

"You may wish it's them." Harvey took out the toothpick and tucked it in his shirt pocket. "Your boss's boss, Rey Curwood, is vacationing at his place on Second Island. You know, our local man of fame, Order of Canada?" He didn't sound very respectful.

"Ah hum." Natalie agreed. "What about him?"

"Seems Brayburn gave him a call, and he's decided to join us. Says he's bored."

Frustration slid down Natalie's throat and pooled in her stomach. "He's coming to keep an eye on me," she said flatly, "if Brayburn called him."

"NO." Harvey said. "You've a terrific track record. Why would he spy on you?"

"Humph. My track record is in other divisions and predates my dance with the explosive. Brayburn is not convinced I'm ready to return to active duty. He warned me he'd be watching."

"Slugs," Harvey muttered. "Don't they know I have your back?"

Nat patted his forearm. "No worries. I know you have my back." She slapped her hand on the car. "No, he doesn't trust me."

She flipped her fingers against her chin. "I guess all I can do is show them I'm fine. No damn way am I going back on disability. I've recovered, and as long as I don't give them reason to doubt me, I'll be around for a long time."

Gravel at the roadside crunched and a fancy car pulled through the gates and rolled silently across the asphalt. Mutt, until then happy to sit, stood and growled. The car engine lingered and died and the driver opened the door. Curwood unfolded his six-foot-something frame from the low-slung car. Mutt's hackles rose accompanied by a grumbling growl.

Nat knelt and wrapped an arm around the dog, putting her face close to his head. "Relax, Mutt. He's a friendly." She whispered an addendum for Mutt's ear only. "Keep your guard up, boy, he may not be as friendly as we think." If she viewed Curwood as the capable officer he was, she might learn something from him. But being watched irked her. She stood as Curwood reached them. *But I can't send him away. I'll have to make do.*

"Good afternoon, sir."

The man with the silver hair and immaculate shirt raised a hand, palm out. "Please. Skip the sir. Call me Rey." The accompanying smile added to his harmless look. Apparently, his innocent look had enticed more than one suspect to trust him when they shouldn't.

She smiled and inclined her head. *But I won't be fooled.*

"Sorry to infringe," he said. "But quite frankly I'm bored. And this is only a vacation. What I'll do when I fully retire, I don't know. I can only stand so many rounds of golf. If you don't mind, I'd like to tag along." He shook hands with Nat first and Harvey second, silently acknowledging her seniority.

"No worries, s…Rey." Natalie gave an inch. *Maybe he really does want to offset boredom. After all, on my medical leave, I cursed inactivity.*

Rey knelt by Mutt and held out his hand, knuckles up. "Hey, boy, I hear you brought home a gift."

Mutt's rear end went into wagging overdrive, and he licked the offered hand.

She gave the dog a look and pursed her lips. *What a sucker for attention. You traitor.*

Harvey pulled out the toothpick and put it back in the opposite corner of his mouth. Whatever he thought, it didn't show on his face. *And I probably should call him Constable or Conrad on the job.*

Curwood patted Mutt's head and stood facing Natalie. "So, what's the story?" His spicy aftershave tickled her nose and she sneezed.

Nat stuck her fingers into her front pockets and glanced at Harvey. "Just got here myself. Constable Conrad, give us what you've got."

"I got a call on my private cell this morning. Adam could hardly get the words out. Mutt went out for his morning business and…"

"Excuse me." Curwood interrupted. "Adam? Mutt? And why your private cell?"

"Adam Mason's dog is Mutt. Adam, his mother Lydia and his younger brother live over the grocery store. Lydia runs it for the owner. I'm Adam's Big Brother so he has my number."

"Ah, I see," Curwood said. "Go on."

"Anyway," Harvey said, "Mutt brought home bones and dumped them in the kitchen. When Adam went to throw them outside, he freaked. His word. Lydia recognized it as a hand and partial arm A few bits were missing, but she pegged it as human."

Curwood turned his attention to the dog now lolling on his side watching a fly buzz past his nose. "Doesn't look too bright, does he?"

Parker defended the dog. "Bright enough when needs be."

"Have you tried letting the dog have his head?" Curwood asked. "And followed him?"

"Of course." Harvey's voice remained neutral. "But he simply headed for another bone, one he'd been given, and settled down for a chew."

"And the ones he found, they were bone only?"

Duh, hadn't Harvey said as much? Natalie held her breath. *Shut up brain. I don't need the snarky comments.*

Harvey answered with his habitual calm. "Pretty much. No flesh."

"What about the old graveyard? It's been around since the 1700s. Maybe a grave, one without a coffin, coughed up its occupant."

Natalie pinched her lips together, and let Harvey continue the lead. Curwood, with his obvious ideas, seemed to be second-guessing her abilities the way Brayburn did. And she didn't trust herself to keep her snippy thoughts to herself.

"Been there," Harvey said curtly, his calm punctured. "No disturbances at all. I took Mutt on the leash and did a sweep pattern search in the woods behind the graveyard but with no results. I've called for some extra feet on the ground." He looked at his watch. "They should be here now. We'll lay out a grid and start into the woods on this side of Westerly Road. Another of Mutt's favorite squirrel chasing haunts."

Curwood opened his mouth once more, not about to give up. "And you don't think he brought it up from the beaches?"

"There's a bit of leaf sticking to it. No sand. No seaweed. Not likely the beach."

Natalie stood back and watched the posturing between the two men. Curwood had the experience and seniority. But Harvey knew the area as well as he knew the lines in the station house ceiling. She scuffed a foot and inspected the tree tops. It might not be her who had to watch out for Curwood.

"And there were no identifying items with the hand?"

"Nothing but a fragment of deciduous leaf."

"Sounds like you've got it covered." Curwood's attempt to be gracious fell a tad into the boss-giving-reluctant-praise mode. "Is it possible to see the bones?"

Harvey shook his head. The toothpick bobbed once.

Nat watched the toothpick. *How does he talk with that thing in there?*

"Nope. Unless you're headed to the *Forensics Investigation Service* in Halifax. Already bagged and at the detachment for transport there."

Curwood took a moment to scan the area, checking behind him as well as in front. Natalie waited. Harvey chewed his toothpick. The boss-man shifted foot-to-foot. "Well, I'd be happy to join the search team."

Harvey's toothpick dipped. Apparently, he was as surprised as her. But she could hardly refuse. *He's pompous enough to think we are delighted to have such an expert on site.* If Brayburn didn't have a microscope on her career, she might have tried to politely refuse. Better to just nod.

Harvey looked at her. "Want to drive up with me and Mutt?" He did not extend the invitation to her superior officer.

Natalie nodded, directing her gaze at Curwood. "Thanks for the offer. See you up on Westerly Road." And she headed for Harvey's car.

Once inside, the two kept their faces forward as Harvey headed out.

"Well, that's our fun for the day," Natalie said.

"Don't let him intimidate you," Harvey said. "Remember I've got your back. He's not going to see anything he can report as questionable."

****

Harvey wheeled the car around the corner onto Westerly Road

and pulled up behind the two squad cars and five officers waiting for them. The Cove's eagle-eyed occupants would be curious. All the cars and men wouldn't go unnoticed. Brayburn may have already released a news bulletin. Until they found more than a few bones, the general public wouldn't pay much attention. Now the locals, they always paid attention.

"Want to make a bet on how long it will be before more people start wandering by?" Parker asked.

"Humph," Harvey responded. "Not on your life. Someone will be delegated to show up. What shall we tell them when they do?"

"We'll fall back on the not-at-liberty-to-say remark," Natalie said. "The fewer people who know about the bones for now, the better. We need to know what we are dealing with first."

"Look, you take lead," Harvey said. "The men are from my detachment, but if you want to impress his nibs, you'll need to head the charge. The boys won't mind."

"Right you are," Natalie said, getting out of the car. Squaring her shoulders, she headed toward the men.

"Hey, Parker, nice to have you back." Handshakes and greetings went the rounds. Each man held a long pole with a pointed end.

"Turner, I see you and the troops are ready for action," she said. She nodded to him. "Good to see you again."

The tall, black man, who usually partnered with Harvey, ducked his head in response. No more than she expected from the man. He was the king of few words.

I could learn a lesson from him. Ever since my concussion, my mouth engaging too soon gets me into trouble. Not a good attribute for an officer.

"We have a large area to search. We'll take it section by section." She pointed south down the road. "I'll take point at the south end. Spread out and keep each other in sight." She looked at the wooded area with its thick brush. "On second thought, let's be no more than an arm's span plus a foot or so apart. If we can manage it." She grinned at them. "We don't expect you to walk through trees." The remark triggered chuckles.

Their laughter died as Rey Curwood's sleek car stopped behind Harvey's and the man got out. Glances shot back and forth, but no one said anything.

Curwood settled a baseball cap on his head and pulled on work gloves as he advanced.

Raised eyebrows asked the question but quickly dropped over passive faces as the senior officer reached them.

Natalie greeted him. "Officer Curwood has offered to give us a hand. Looking at the dense woods here, we're going to need all the eye-power we can get." She accepted a pole from Turner.

"Rey," she said, setting a casual tone, "you take the other end." She pointed to the corner where Westerly Road met Gerber's Lane.

Harvey handed Curwood a pole, and Curwood turned to the men. "Look for anywhere this mutt might have dug. Or indents in the soil indicating settling over an impromptu grave. Abnormalities in the greenery or flowers showing richer soil could mark a buried body. Officer Conrad informed me trees are down after the weekend storm. We might be looking for something under upturned roots. Keep your eyes open. Sing out if you see something."

Parker turned away and faced Turner. The slight flicker in his eyes had her grinning. "You heard the man," she said and marched toward the ditch. Once they were lined up, they scrambled across and into the brush.

Harvey paused. "Looks like there might have been a road or path here." He pointed to where there were more bushes than trees. Harvey turned the dog loose. "Keep an eye on the dog. If we're lucky, he will head for where he got the bones."

Sun leaked through the foliage and broiled Nat's head. Branches scraped her arms and weeds tangled her feet. Mutt sniffed rocks, anointed a tree and carried on, his tongue lolling out. He only showed real action when a squirrel chattered in a tree top. Natalie checked the line and edged around a spreading spruce. The brush gave way to an even thinner patch. She looked up. Ahead, she spied a gray, slanted roof. *A roof? An unknown building here, in the woods?*

She whistled to get Harvey's attention. The whole group stopped. "Constable Conrad, did you know there is a building in here?"

He pulled off a work glove and swiped his hand over his dripping forehead. "No one lives in there. I don't know what the building is."

"I'll be damned." Curwood's voice rose over the trees. "I can't believe the old house is real."

Heads turned toward him, but only his shoulders showed.

"I remember hearing about a vacant house from the locals years ago." His voice carried through and over the thicket. "They used it for a fort, and later," he added, "as a hang-out for underage drinking. I haven't thought about it in years."

Natalie looked back and realized that no tall trees blocked the view toward the road. "So the area with just bushes might be an old driveway?"

"Could be. I don't remember anyone saying how they got to the house."

An old house. And he hadn't thought of it? Seemed like something one would remember, especially since they were looking for a possible corpse.

"The house might explain a lot, including the potential body," she said. "Back in the day, people did have home graveyards." Mutt plunked down beside her, panting. "Hey, who has water for our intrepid lead dog?"

Turner appeared in a gap in the bushes and passed over a water bottle. "Thanks." Natalie dripped water onto the dog's lolling tongue, and he lapped it in.

Mutt turned from his water fountain, and she stood. "Okay, troops. Let's see what we find. And don't assume that what we are looking for is at the house. Due diligence, people."

Curiosity provided energy and, although still checking, everyone moved a little faster. Only moments later Natalie stepped into an area that gave her a clearer view of the house. First Harvey and then the others joined her at what might have been a lawn area for the house.

Mutt yapped, and Nat bent and ruffled his ears. "What is it, boy? Do you remember where you got the bones?"

Mutt raced off, rounded a maple tree and disappeared. Six sets of feet trampled after him.

His tail wagging, Mutt scrabbled his front paws into a gaping hole. Tree roots, dirt clinging to the raw wooden fingers arched over him. The trunk stretched away and rested on what looked like a covered deck.

Harvey knelt beside the dog and snapped on his leash. Pulling him back, he looked over at Natalie. "I think we found what we're looking for."

"Not too close," Curwood ordered, even though the men stood well back. He himself moved a few steps past them and knelt, peering into the hole. "Looks like Conrad is right. I see another bone." He inched back, stood and pulled off his hat and gloves. Like Harvey earlier, he wiped sweat from his brow.

Natalie crossed her arms and pinched her lips together. *I won't confront him. Even if he's taking over.*

Mutt strained to reach his prize. The men who had water, drank. And they all avoided Curwood.

Well, damn it all anyway. Should I be happy there's a case or worried I won't figure things out?

She drew a deep breath and watched Curwood. Did he know more about this place than he'd professed to remember? She shook off the thought. *He's only assessing everything.*

He shook himself and blinked rapidly before turning to her. "We'll need to cordon this off. At least these trees will give something to tie the tape to. And we'll need more than tape if the weather changes." He folded his gloves and stuck them into his hat. "And you'll need permissions as well as other paper work." His words erupted like popping corn kernels. "FIS will need notification. It's been a busy summer for them." He looked up.

Natalie held up her hand. *Enough already. This is my case.* "Yes, I know. A tent, the procedures, everything. Thanks for your help." She paused and waited until he faced her. "Since you know the history, it must be quite a shock to find out there's a body here."

Rey dragged his hand down over his mouth. "Sorry. Too many years in charge." He raised a hand, palm out apologetically. "I'll back off, leave the scene and the paper work to you." He shot a glance at the open hole in the ground. "I wonder how long it's been there."

"We'll find out," Natalie said. "What else do you know about the property?"

He shook his head. "Not much. I haven't been around here since I joined the police force back in 1969." He punched the gloves in his hat. "A lifetime ago. Whether or not another generation used it, I have no idea."

"Understood. We'll handle it." She shook his hand. "Thanks again, and if you remember anything more, you know how to find me."

Curwood smiled. "That's usually my line. I'll give the past some thought. And I'd appreciate updates," he said. "Maybe we could do it over a meal?"

"We'll be in touch." But a meal? Not going to happen. Any questions she had for him would be professionally handled.

Rey accepted her answer and turned, making his way around the big maple. No one moved or spoke until the crashing in the bushes ended. He'd reached the road.

A phone rang into the silence, and they all reached for their cells. Laughter ensued, breaking the tension left behind by Curwood. One of the assisting officers got the call.

"Right, we're on our way." He ended the call. "Come on, you two, accident up on the 103. Duty calls." The three men nodded to Harvey, saluted Natalie and left.

"Turner and I can run the tape," Harvey said. "How much area do you think?"

Natalie pulled out her phone. "Make it wide and long. Who knows where parts might be. Over the years, root growth and water could have moved smaller items. I'll call Brayburn and update him." She made a face. "Hope he's not unhappy about Curwood abandoning us."

****

Brayburn answered on the third ring.

"Good news and bad news," she said. "We found more bones. Maybe an entire body. Hard to say until it's excavated." She added details of the house, tree and old yard. "Thanks for sending over Chief Superintendent Curwood," she added. "Turns out he knows about the house."

An expletive reverberated through the phone. Brayburn added an indistinguishable sound. "And the bad news?"

"This is going to take lots of excavation, delicate work probably. We'll need an M.E., a tech or two, maybe some students to do the grunt work and the van."

Brayburn huffed into the phone, and his breath whistled in her ear. "Bloody great, we don't have time or manpower for a long, drawn-out case." He sighed and settled to business. "Come in tomorrow with all the details and photos…you do have pictures?"

Duh, do you think? She kept the words in her head. *Is he fishing for a reason to pull me off this?*

When she didn't answer he went on. "Right, you have photos. Let's see what you've got and what's on the docket here and we'll decide what to do with this."

Damn, he is looking to side-rail the investigation. And yet, knowing the case load, she couldn't blame him.

Brayburn continued planning. "I'll get things started here and call Zhang over at FIS. You, I'll see tomorrow." He hung up.

An instant later, her phone rang. Brayburn again. "Who owns the land?"

"Greg Cunningham and Devon Ritcey."

"Any trouble getting permission to excavate?"

"Doubt it. You know him. Cunningham served on the force for years and then started a security company."

"Oh, right, his partner is Logan. Good enough." Once again, Brayburn skipped a good-bye and hung up.

She tucked the phone into her pocket and retrieved her camera. The tape, now wound around trees and bushes, effectively cordoned off the area visually. She wanted pictures showing the positioning of all the tapes. Although who would show up to see it, she didn't know.

Yes, you do. If the Cove residents get curious, they'll be up here taking a look.

But as long as it wasn't tourists, they'd respect the yellow line.

What I don't know is who might have information about the deceased. She couldn't imagine any of the old timers, killing and burying someone. If it even was a murder. *I shouldn't jump to conclusions.* Historically, they might have buried Grandma at home and moved on. She edged around the perimeter, taking out twists in the tape and lining it up parallel to the ground. *If the skeleton is old enough to be some one's great-grandmother, I'll be happy.*

On the other hand, the graveyard just up the road had been in use since the 1700s, and not since the early 1970s. That left quite a time window. Heat increased her tension and the tiny, always present, headache threatened to blossom. She needed to focus, eat something and, as much as she hated taking meds, she needed her pills. *Five trees, four singing birds, and one annoyed squirrel*. The tension subsided and with it, the lurking pain.

"Well, boys," she said, "looks like we're done here. Your shift must be over. Let's talk to Devon Ritcey and after, I'll buy you some supper up in Bridgewater. I'm not ready for the questions we'd get at the café."

Natalie turned and picked her way around trees and over bushes, and headed for the car. Harvey and Turner willingly collected their gear and followed.

Tired didn't come close to describing her physical and mental state. She hadn't spent that much time on her feet, never mind out in the fresh air, in months. *As a first day back in the field, it has been quite eventful.*

CHAPTER THREE

Skeletons and flames haunted Natalie's dreams, and she greeted the morning with gritty and itchy eyes. Outside, haze lingered over the ocean waiting for sun's rays to burn it off. The day promised to be clear and hot. Her morning meditation, another prescription to keep her panic attacks at bay, helped, but not by much. *And Brayburn will expect me first off.* She made it to the office, parked and made the long trek down the second-floor hall. Her heart tripped triple time. She filled her lungs, held in the air and sucked in her midriff. When the heart-tripping stopped, she exhaled audibly through pursed lips and entered.

Brayburn looked up, eyeing her as she crossed the open space toward his office. He nodded at the chair across from him.

As if I didn't know enough to sit. He and Rey Curwood have more than the police background in common. Control freaks. Natalie managed to keep her face calm. Ever since the explosion, and the accompanying cynical voice in her head, keeping her thoughts from spilling into verbal form became a full-time job.

Her boss tipped his head at his computer. "I've finished reading your report. And I printed the scanned permission letter from Devon Ritcey. Cunningham didn't sign?"

"He's away on a job in Europe. He'll email you a letter directly."

Her boss tapped a few keys. "I see the scene is cordoned off. The forensics people will get out there today and set up a tent. Although managing with those trees in the way won't be easy."

No kidding.

He shuffled paper. "The forensics people will excavate the bones and help ID the body. Although the bones are old, this is a new case."

She smiled slightly and inclined her head. *Good, a new case gets investigated now.*

"We'll give this two more days. Depends on what forensics comes up with. Find out what you can. We won't proceed further unless we find strong evidence of murder. Even then, it may have to wait. Current cases still take priority. The proper forms will be available by the end of the day. I'll email them. You can stay on while the M.E. makes the first assessment." He glanced up. "But don't count on staying any longer."

Nat took her time answering. She didn't need him to tell her how to do her job. *But it is as it is.* "Yes, sir."

"Now, get moving. The M.E. and her team will on the site tomorrow." He picked up a pen. "You have today to talk to people. Find the oldest residents and get started."

Yes, sir, Thank you for pointing it out. What had the head blow done to her thinking? She'd never made so many silent comebacks before.

"It's probably an old skeleton and a natural death."

Gee, don't sound so hopeful.

Natalie squelched the mental rejoinder and stood. She shouldn't be so snippy. *He's only doing his job.* At least she'd kept her comments off her tongue. An improvement over blurting out things as she had during the first weeks after the head trauma. Turning, she sped across the open area to the exit.

A half an hour later, she had her foot firmly pressed on the gas pedal. Her pulse raced and pounded in her ears. *No way am I slowing down.*

With only two days to gather preliminary information, she had no time to waste. By the time she crossed the bridge to the island and turned right toward Caleb's Cove, she'd compiled her action list. First, she'd visit the site, compare photos with existing tapes and make sure no one had tampered with the site.

She blew past the buses at the café and Lem and his group of tourists in the graveyard. She parked by three cars on Westerly Road, grabbing her tablet and, she stepped out to the whine of power saws. The sparsely wooded area from yesterday now gaped open, bracketed on either side by stacked brush. Following the sounds, she found Harvey, Jackson Ritcey and three others busy with chain saws.

Natalie hailed Harvey. "Hey, what's up?"

All three men shut down their saws. Harvey wiped his shirt sleeve across his forehead. "Hot work," he said.

Natalie grinned. "So I see. Isn't this your day off?" she asked.

He pushed up his safety goggles. "Devon suggested it. She doesn't want a horde cutting through by the main house and up the lawn. A clear-cut here will provide the easiest access."

"Makes sense. And you all volunteered?" She waved a hand including the other three.

"We did, sort of," Jackson said. "My sister doesn't take no for an answer."

Hart Harris, a medical student working for the summer, stepped forward, a grin on his face. "I came because it gave me an excuse to be close to the investigation."

Natalie shook her head. "Men. However, clear-cutting is a good move. Carry on. I'm going to check the site."

Harvey set down his saw. "About the site," he said and fell into step beside her. "I think there was a visitor last night."

Natalie sped up and rounded the maple into the cordoned area. She stopped and peered at the open hole and area.

"Go a bit closer," Harvey said, pointing. "There's dirt knocked into the hole that wasn't there yesterday. I checked with the photos we took. And," he said, pointing to the area closest to the roots, "it does look like someone did some extra digging."

She moved forward and opened the tablet, flipped to her photos and made a comparison. "Damn, someone or something disturbed things." She knelt and examined the ground around the hole. "The earth is soft enough for animal or human prints to show. It didn't rain here last night, did it?" She looked around the enclosed area and down at the footprints made the day before by Curwood. "Someone with the same sized shoe could have come across the grass before stepping in the indents left by Curwood." She snapped pictures.

"If that someone had the exact size of shoe, they could have. Anything smaller would have left extra imprints. But if they were slightly bigger, the shoes might have simply enlarged what was already there. We have photos as we left it yesterday. Forensics should be able to match those with what we have today." He looked into the tree tops. "I don't think birds would have bothered the site. Besides the marks are too extensive for birds."

"True." Natalie sighed. "Either the curious were looking for souvenirs or someone is concerned about what is in this grave."

She took more pictures. "I'll email these to FIS. But we'd better watch this place closely. If you lot have to leave, you'd better get Turner or the rookie over here to keep an eye on things. We'll worry about overnight later."

She led the way back to the work area. "You don't think Adam would have come for a look? Do you?"

"Doubt it," Harvey said. "He doesn't know where to come."

"Probably not," Nat said. "But I'll talk to him anyway. He's curious enough to want to know what's going on. Better we should tell him than have him come poking around." She made her good-byes and headed to her car.

Time to talk to Adam. He probably wanted to ask at least a dozen questions. The kid wanted to know everything. *He'll make a good detective one day if he wants to.*

She headed north and pulled into an empty grocery store lot. The bell over the door shattered a stillness inside. Lydia came around the center stacks to greet her.

"Officer Parker, good to see you. We've been wondering what happened about the, um." She glanced away. "Bones Mutt found. The news didn't say anything specific and Adam wants to call Harvey. I made him wait. Figured you don't need him bugging you."

"Thanks," Natalie said. "Is Adam here?"

Lydia looked over her shoulder. "He and Kane are out back with Mutt." She sighed and shook her head. "They are probably over in the graveyard. Ever since the dog came home with the bones, Adam has been talking about dead people. I'm not sure what to tell him." A deep sigh rolled up from her middle. "And Dave Lamont gave the boys a metal detector. They spend hours using it."

"Not surprising." Nat smiled. "They're curious. I'll go have a chat."

The clanging bell announced a new arrival. Lily Gerber, the store owner, joined them.

"Natalie. Saw your car. After the parade yesterday, everyone is wondering what's up."

"So, two police cars make a parade?"

"Well, two squad cars, your car, Harvey's car and Curwood's car. To top it off, they released a brief report on bones, possibly human, found on the island. Yes, parade or not, we are curious."

Natalie whistled. "The eyes of the Cove at work. The bones are human and we've found a possible gravesite. A team will be down to investigate, and when I have more information, I'll let you know."

"Darn, I suppose it's the 'ongoing investigation' comment. And here I am hoping to get the scoop." Lily leaned into her crutch. "But I guess I'll have to wait?"

"Yes." Natalie said. "Now, I'm going to talk to Adam." She looked at Lydia. "I'll send Kane in, okay? He's a bit young for graves and bones."

"I'd appreciate that," Lydia said, "he's prone to bad dreams as it is."

Natalie found Adam and Kane headed back from the graveyard with Mutt dancing around them. She waited for them by the picnic table.

"Adam, I need to talk to you," she said. She gave them each a hug and looked at Kane. "You head in and see your mom. Adam and I have official business to discuss."

Kane looked at her. "Is it about that *thing*?" He scrunched his eyes at the last word.

She nodded.

"Then, thin-kin, I'm out and about from here, dear." Kane gave his usual rhyming statement and ran for the door.

Natalie knelt by Mutt and scratched his ears. "You dug up a pretty kettle of fish, didn't you boy?" The dog put one paw on her shoulder and licked her face. She patted him then moved to sit beside Adam at the picnic table.

He placed his metal detector on the table top and, tucking his hands under his thighs, tilted forward, staring at the ground. "Those bones are from a person? Right?"

"Yes, but they're old. They won't belong to anyone we knew."

Adam considered the information. "Are there more? Bones, like?"

"Between you and me, yes. But we are not telling everyone

yet."

"Okay." He turned and looked at her. "Where are they?"

So he hadn't been up at the dig site.

"Over in the woods." She added basic details about the tree roots and old house.

"Are you going to dig them up?"

"Not me. The Medical Examiner will arrive tomorrow and a forensic team will carefully remove the bones."

He rocked forward and back, digesting what she'd said. "What's a Medical Examiner?"

"The M.E. is a doctor…"

His head snapped around. "Why do bones need a doctor?"

She hid her smile. "Bones get a special doctor, one who studies bones for information."

"Like on the show, Bones? But I thought they were path, uh, path-ol-o-gists."

"You're correct. The Chief Medical Examiner is a pathologist."

"So they'll be able to tell if it is a man? And how old? And everything?"

"Exactly."

"That's really cool." Adam pulled his hands out from under him. "And will you tell me what they find out?"

"You bet. Actually, Dr. Zhang is the M.E. Once she's done, I'll see if she'll meet you."

"Oh man, oh man." Adam jumped off the bench. "Super cool. Wait till I go back to school. For once when the teacher asks that dumb question about what you did on your vacation, I'll have something no one could guess. I bet I win the most interesting summer vacation." He punched air with both hands. "Thanks, Constable Parker."

She laughed. "You can call me Natalie if you like."

He shook his head. "Mom says we can't call adults by their first names." He thought. "It's like, um, not respectful. But I could call you Miss Natalie if that's okay."

Natalie stood. "Miss Natalie works. But now, I've got to get going. You can tell people Mutt found the bones, but remember, all the other details are still a secret. I'll let you know as soon as you can tell people about it."

Adam's face fell. "Darn." But he nodded and stuck out his hand. "I won't tell. Here, I'll shake on it."

She shook his hand. "Thanks, Adam. Talk to you soon.

****

The second day Brayburn had allowed for investigating dawned clear and windy. The sun played hide and seek with the clouds, but the temperature promised scorching heat. The shade at the dig site would be welcome.

Parker exited the café, her travel mug in her hand and sipped as she waited. Two cars and a dark navy van pulled into the lot. The driver's window on the lead vehicle lowered, and Dr. Zhang waved to Parker.

"We're here. It's a small place, eh?"

"Too small," Parker replied. "Not enough people, or action, to get lost in."

Zhang laughed. "Ah, so that's why I feel like I'm being watched. I am."

Parker agreed and pointed to her own vehicle. "Follow me, the site is five minutes from here." She glanced around. "Who am I kidding, everything in the Cove is five minutes from here." The numerous vehicles formed a real parade, at least by island measurement. How long would it be before locals moved from looking on to demanding answers?

On Westerly Road, Dr. Zhang joined Parker by the ditch. Sturdy planks covered new fill and gave access to the newly cleared trail through the trees. "Looks like you're ready for us."

"Constable Conrad and some local men cleared this yesterday. I hope they've made it level enough for you to get the van in. I'm guessing it would make your job easier."

The older woman nodded and turned slightly to watch the others joining them. "These two, Rob and Karen, are our two most experienced techs. These three," she said sweeping them together with her wave, "are in their last semester of the forensics course at the Mount and were sent to do grunt work and learn."

Natalie shook hands all around and pointed to the new roadway. "This way, folks."

Rob, the van driver, checked the ground as he went. "Looks okay," he said, "we can get the van in." He tipped his head and looked up at the maple tree. "Is our site much farther?"

"Around the tree," Natalie said, leading the way along the path created by busy feet. At the barrier, she stopped. "There it is."

Dr. Zhang ducked under the tape and walked closer, being careful not to disturb the sidewalls on the hole. "Goodness, the remains certainly are embedded. Any idea which way the head points?"

"Not a clue. Once we found it, we backed off. Figured this is a job for the experts." Nat stayed outside the tape. "You can take some cuts and figure it out, can't you?"

The M. E. stood. "True, but so much easier and neater if we know when we start."

Natalie joined Dr. Zhang. "I am hoping for a bare bones skeleton and natural cause of death with the burial having happened a hundred years ago." She glanced around, checking for unwanted listeners. "But we think we had a visitor here last night. Looks like they did some poking around." She indicated the footprints and disturbed dirt. "We're hoping you can confirm that. There are before and after photos."

"We'll do our best." The doctor looked at the building. "Do you know how old the house is?"

"The current owners have documents showing when this lot and the house were added to the main estate. I think it was in the 1920s or '30s. But, it existed before then, so we still don't know exactly when it was built. However, it hasn't been lived in since the late sixties."

Dr. Zhang pursed her lips. "So this skeleton *might* be over one hundred years old. But, I don't think so. The partial hand and arm we have suggested it's younger." She rubbed her hands together and grinned. "An excellent puzzle for sure."

Karen and the three students came around the maple tree carrying gear. Rob had pulled the van in as far as he could before he joined them.

"Rob, brush the loose dirt off the area around the protruding bone, would you," Zhang said. "We need to get the skeleton's orientation." She donned shoe covers and paper coveralls.

Rob, garbed the same, extracted two brushes from his gear. Kneeling on a mat beside the roots, he steadied himself with one hand on the tree trunk and carefully brushed aside dirt. Within minutes more bone lay exposed, and he stopped.

"Pelvic area," he said. "Looks like the head is that way," he said, pointing toward the southeast into the tree roots, "and it looks like the body is buried on its side. Not a usual burial position."

Natalie leaned in to check the bones. *No coffin and a body on its side. Definitely confirmation that this isn't a regular burial.*

"Good work," Dr. Zhang said. "Let's get at it."

Karen, equipped with a high-end camera, started shooting still shots. Rob set up a movie recorder and sighted through it, adjusting until satisfied it would capture their work.

Dr. Zhang crouched by the open area. "The upper body is really entwined with the roots," she said. "We'll start with the legs." Accepting a brush from Rob, she set to work.

Car doors slammed in the distance and minutes later Harvey and Turner arrived, carrying water. "Thought you'd need these." Harvey set the water in the shade and pulled out a bottle, twisted off the cap and upended it. He downed the whole thing without a stop. "Ah, so much better." He picked up another and brought it to Natalie. "What have we got so far?"

She accepted the water. "We've uncovered the bottom half. Apparently, they'd have preferred starting at top, but the torso and head are caught in roots."

Turner stood, catching shade from the maple tree. He too drank water, although not as exuberantly as his partner. "Any pronouncements?" A whole speech for the often silent officer.

Natalie shook her head. "As much as I want to know, I don't want to know. I'm still holding out for grandma from the last century."

Dr. Zhang heard her and leaving the dig, scooped up a water and joined Natalie. "I can give you an update."

Natalie looked skyward and back down. "Let's hear it."

"The pelvis is female. And given the belt buckle and the denim scrap we've found, I'd hazard a guess she wore jeans. But don't hold me to it. But, probably not grandma." She paused to enjoy some water. "Learning how old the tree is will give us a time estimate. The bones and roots are entangled, suggesting the tree grew after she was buried." She glanced at the tree. "We'll get a slice of the trunk later. I don't want to start cutting until we have Miss Doe extracted."

Natalie sighed. "Well, damn anyway. Finding the poor lady is bad enough. Thinking there's someone who might have known her, is worse. Because I'll bet you a month's pay she is related to someone living in the Cove."

Harvey snorted. "No one who knows the place will take your bet. Everyone knows everyone, and their ancestors, and in many cases are related even if it is back six generations."

Dr. Zhang put her empty water bottle back in the flat. "I don't envy you the interviews. The bones will tell me stories. But skeletons don't cry. Makes my job a bit easier." She pulled on her gloves and returned to her grisly task.

CHAPTER FOUR

Natalie pulled out her tablet and leaned against a tree. *Lists, I need lists and a plan if I'm going to make progress before Brayburn pulls us off this case.* Using the computers at the security office for searches would save time. And talking to the older residents might be fast and effective. *Let's see—Mrs. Gerber and Lem for sure.* Her phone interrupted her process.

Devon. She shut off the tablet and slid it into its shoulder bag. "What's up?" Natalie asked.

"You stole my question," Devon replied. "As well as the question of half the people in the Cove. Kelsey and Lily are here and they claim to represent most of the other Cove inhabitants. All those vehicles rolling through town has people curious. Everyone is waiting with bated breath for information. They seem to think they have a proprietary right to more details than the news is giving the world at large."

Sounds about right for the local thinking. Why can't everyone stay home and ignore us? A breeze stirred the leaves overhead and sunlight flashed in her eyes, stabbing her headache. The upcoming investigation, the questions, and finding this woman's identity wouldn't be easy. Natalie pushed away from the tree. She might as well get started.

"When will they realize they have to wait like everyone else?"

"Thought you might say that. Turn around."

Natalie turned. The three women waved to her from the clear-cut area. Kelsey lugged a camping jug. Devon carried a grocery bag. Lily leaned on her crutch with a big smile on her face.

Snapping her phone shut, Natalie watched the three women approach. *I'm doing okay and this crew shows up to complicate things.*

"I thought everyone could use food and beverage," Devon said. "So, we brought some."

"Thoughtful," Natalie said, not hiding her sarcasm. "And is that the only reason you came?" She lifted one eyebrow in her best inquisitional look.

Devon set the jug down beside the flat of water. "Well, we do want to know what's going on. And this is my land. And you know we're good with secrets and," she said, fluttering her fingers, "finding answers."

Natalie let a laugh ripple through her thoughts. She'd summed it up nicely. But did Devon have to sound so gleeful? "This is not a case for 'The Touched by Murder Club'." She downed her water and headed toward the women. That darn club had butted into enough investigations. It didn't help that they usually helped.

She passed Harvey on her way. "And so it starts," she muttered. "I'll settle the natives, you keep on with those photos."

She raised her voice. "Lunch, every one." She looked at Kelsey. "What's in the blue jug?"

"Lemonade."

"Did you order us up a portable potty house?"

Devon laughed. "I left the number four cabin unlocked for washroom use."

At least, Devon had been thinking.

"Now," Devon said, handing off sandwiches to Rob while Kelsey passed others to Harvey. "I know you have a skeleton in the hole."

Ah yes, she knew from the request for permission to dig on her land. And she always shared everything with Kelsey.

"You know all there is to know."

"Come on," Lily added. "You must know something new by now."

Natalie saw an opening to shift the conversation. Lily would have been living in the Cove about forty-plus years ago. She might know something that would help. Worth a shot. "Lily, when did you leave here for Montreal?"

"1969," Lily replied easily. "The first week in August. We were headed for Woodstock but we didn't make it. Got sidetracked in Montreal."

"Do you remember if anyone disappeared before you left?"

Lily shook her head. "Why, do they think the body got here around then?" She peered around Natalie at the dig site.

"Maybe. No fixed date yet."

Devon took a step toward Dr. Zhang.

"Hold it." Nat pointed at Devon. "No questions. This is an ongoing investigation. We ask the questions. You lot answer them."

"But…"

Natalie held up a hand. "No buts. The skeletal remains are female. Undetermined time, cause, and method of death. End of story for now. Thank you for the refreshments, but as a bribe for information they are not going to work."

Dr. Zhang laughed and covered her mouth for a moment. She motioned with her hand at her crew. "Come, eat and then back to work. We need to find out the time, cause and method of death before this crew dies of curiosity."

"Now you know as much as I do," Natalie said to the three women. "But no discussion past here, right?"

"If you insist," Devon said. "But I can tell Greg, can't I?"

"Yes, you can tell him," Natalie allowed. As the property owner, an ex-police officer and a man an ocean away, he was a safe person to tell.

Kelsey executed a dance move. "And I can tell Sam."

Sighing, Parker capitulated. "Tell Sam, too." She turned to Lily. "I suppose you want to tell Dave?" *More retired police officers. How did they all end up here?*

Lily nodded. "Yes. He'll keep it under wraps."

Natalie muttered a curse. "Keeping it under wraps isn't the problem. It's the osmosis effect in this place. People seem to know things even when everyone else swears up and down they didn't tell."

The other three exchanged glances. She turned her back on them and rolled her eyes. She rounded on them again. "Look, this is important. It's probable someone killed this girl. The surprise effect might help in figuring out who."

Devon raised a hand and crossed her heart. "It'll be a secret for the six of us to know…and you …and Harvey and Turner…and the team and…."

Natalie closed her eyes and shook her head before answering. "I get your point. Do the best you can." She turned to Lily. "If you do remember anything pertinent from back in the sixties, you'll call." A directive, not a question. "Is your mother home?"

"She'll be there later. Right now she's over to her cousin's place."

"Good, let me know as soon as she gets back. If anyone remembers anything, it'll be her. Maybe I can block the osmosis effect."

"Good luck with that," Lily said.

The three women retreated under Natalie's brow-furrowed glare.

Harvey and Turner passed over the camera. "If you're here for the duration," he said, "we'll head for the detachment and some paperwork." He tapped her shoulder. "Talk to you later." He and Turner left.

Natalie returned to the maple tree. With the sun in the west, the shadows were lengthening. Evening came much quicker here on the coast than in central Alberta where she'd grown up.

She turned and looked the house. Only a few trees blocked her view. *A teen hangout, a fort for younger kids, and before then, someone's home.* It could be one hundred years old. Eventually, she'd go and check inside, for what she wasn't sure. But her instincts said she should.

Dr. Zhang approached. "We're making decent progress." She gestured at the growing root pile. "We sliced off the roots we could. The ones inside the skeleton will stay for now. We can do a cut-down and take the whole works out intact." She looked back at her work. "We're up to the shoulders," she said. "The skull will need to come out with a good-sized block, dirt, roots and all. With the skeleton on its side, sorting out what's what is tricky. But we've got it."

"Can you tell how she died?"

Zhang shook her head. "Once we do the final cut-down and get her into the van, we'll start to find answers."

"Today?"

"No answers until tomorrow. Rob will sleep in the trailer tonight so there is someone on site. I have to get back to headquarters." She looked at her watch. "The other four have rooms in Bridgewater. Tomorrow they'll sift the dirt for the grave and surrounding area. It's often surprising what we find. And then we are out of here." She turned to her team. "Another hour kiddos, and we'll call it a day." Bracing her hand on her lower back, she stretched into a hyper extension. "Don't worry. We WILL get answers."

The team worked in rhythm, poking, sweeping and exposing bone. Tomorrow she might be reeled back into the office by Brayburn. Natalie crossed her fingers. Having a murder victim and a disturbed site might convince him to keep the case open. *I need this case. I need to let them know I'm ready for work.*

****

Natalie ate supper with Grace and Devon. Vie took Rob's out to him. The rest of the team had headed for their lodgings in Bridgewater.

Her phone rang as she finished a delicious meat pie.

"Mom's home," Lily said. "And expecting you to visit."

"Thanks, do you think she'll have cookies?"

"What do you think," Lily retorted. "Mom always has cookies." Natalie laughed.

She opted to walk the short distance up Gerber's Lane to Mrs. Gerber's and found her hovering by the door. Dressed in boot-cut jeans and a burgundy sweater, the eighty-six-year-old could have passed for seventy. Her energy, as legendary as her cookies, belied her age.

"Come in, come in. I hear you have a story to tell me and some questions." Her eyes sparkled. "More mysterious happenings. I can't wait." She ushered Nat into her sitting parlor and produced a tray with teapot, cups, and cookies. "Tea without cookies isn't appealing," she said. "And homemade cookies are the best."

"Come now, Mrs. G. Don't be modest. I think what folks say is that yours are the best."

Mrs. G. blew a raspberry, but she looked pleased.

"Did you have a good visit with your cousin?" Manners went a long way in the Cove.

"Yes. But cut the chitchat, I want to know what is going on. Is it about the old house? Did you find a crime? Did a wall fall down and reveal a body?"

Natalie laughed. "Slow down. Obviously, you've heard that something is happening."

"Course I did. I stopped at the store for milk. Everyone is curious." She sighed. "And I suppose there aren't many left who know anything about the old days." With a small shake, she refocused on the teapot and poured. "The house has been there for as long as I remember. Lem must have something at the museum to tell you the age."

Mrs. Gerber passed Natalie the cup and pushed the cookie plate closer to her. "Meanwhile, let me see what MY brain can recall." She pinched her lower lip between thumb and forefinger.

"Jeremy Bockner bought the land right after the war, the second one. He set to building the big house about 1948. He faced a huge job. Back then they either had to come across the flats at low tide or bring supplies across by barge. The construction provided much-needed work after the war. My Ivan worked there. That's when I met him." She smiled, and her face took on a distant look. "I had just turned fifteen. We kept company for five years before my parents agreed to us marrying."

She set down her teacup. "But you want to know about the house. It stood vacant by the time I was born in 1931. Not sure exactly how for how long. My mother talked about the storekeeper who had lived there. His store was right on the waterfront, where the boathouse is now, because people traveled by boat between the islands. But after those hurricanes..." Her voice trailed off.

"The August Gales," Natalie said. "Devon mentioned them."

"Big storms, hurricanes really and they always hit in August. 1926 and 27 were well remembered. One hundred and thirty-three men went down with the fishing boats. Made a huge hole in the fleet along the coast here." She worried her hands in her lap. "My grandfather and his brother went down with their ship." She shook her head. "My mother said it wasn't the same after they died. The fisheries failed as well and so many families, left without the men to provide, moved away." She looked up. "Including the shopkeeper and his daughter, a nurse. I think." She stopped long enough to eat a cookie.

Natalie sighed. "Doesn't sound like anything sinister happened. Sad but not sinister."

"True," Mrs. Gerber said. She thought for a moment and tsked. "Now you know everything I remember about those days. I don't even know the shopkeeper's name." She looked over. "Have you been over to the Lahave Museum? Or to the cairn on the other island."

"Not yet," Natalie said.

Mrs. Gerber washed down her cookie and cradled her cup between her hands. "So there may have been people in the house now and again. But I'm not sure. They finished construction on the big house later in the fifties. Mr. Bockner's caretaker and his family lived in the old house. A Mr. and Mrs. Roberts and their daughter, Gloria. They updated and repaired the house. But they left in late spring 1968. I remember it was the year before my Lily left."

"Do you know why the Roberts family left, or where they went?" Nat paused. "And, is there any chance the daughter died and was buried there for some reason?"

"No. We saw them all again later. But, in the beginning, they left without a word. Simply hauled their belongings to the dock and left on a barge." Mrs. G. wagged a finger. "Just a minute, they'd moved into the big house earlier. There was trouble with plumbing and Mr. Bockner didn't want to spend more money on the old house."

"They left it vacant?" Natalie asked.

"Yes. The trees grew and hid it and people forgot it." She nodded, a glint in her eye. "I'll bet there were a few parties here in the summers. A place for the teens to go when it rained."

"Mrs. G. you have a good memory. Thanks for helping."

The older woman sniffed. "Not much else to do here except remember old stories." She cocked her head and smiled. "At least, not before Devon and Greg came back."

Natalie joined her in a chuckle. A murderer, a crazy killer and a kidnapper over the past six or seven years livened the place up for sure, but not in a good way. "I suppose we have to blame it all on Caleb's curse."

"Pshaw. That old legend." Mrs. Gerber waved the suggestion away with a hand. "Now what can you tell me? Quid pro quo and all."

Natalie started with the find. "We've found a body buried near the old house." She gave Mrs. G. the bare information. "So I'm wondering about the times before and after the Roberts family lived there. Did anyone disappear? Did anything odd happen? Either here on the island or on the mainland nearby?"

"Humph. Let me see. I don't remember my mother saying anything about anyone disappearing." She snorted. "And you can bet if it happened, the quilting club would have talked about it." She shook her head, her face sober. "My Lily went off with that no … that husband in the spring of 1969." She sighed and crossed her arms over her middle. "And there were the two girls who ran away in August. The young didn't want to stay on the island. So many left for school or a job and most never returned."

She'd need specifics about those who left, but first, she needed context. "What went on here in the sixties?"

"Probably like the sixties everywhere. There were teenagers on Second Island. Summer people." She sniffed. "And hippies who carried tents and gear across the flats at low tide and set up in the campground or in clearings around the island. The café was new and had an outside dance stage. We had some great times. And the kids had huge beach parties with Wacky Tabacky as we called it. Never been as lively around here since."

Great details to mine for information, but Natalie wanted to know who was buried on the hill. "Who were the other two girls you mentioned leaving?"

"Amara and Gloria. Quite the pair." A smile twitched her lips. "What friends they were."

Natalie puckered her brow. "I thought Gloria moved away?"

"She came back for the summer the next year and stayed with the Krauses."

"Why the Krauses?" Natalie asked.

"Amara was a Krause. So that's why Gloria stayed there." Mrs. Gerber coughed and pulling out a tissue, dabbed at her tears. "She was my niece."

"Gloria was your niece?"

"No, no. Amara was."

"Ah. I get it. So was she Lenya's sister?"

"Yes, her older sister."

"And you are sure the girls left?"

"Oh yes. No doubt." Mrs. Gerber nodded vigorously. "They'd been talking about seeing the world, or at least Woodstock. When they were gone, everyone looked for them. Mr. and Mrs. Krause notified the police. There wasn't a sign of them." She blew her nose and blinked away tears. "That is until Gloria's body washed up on shore later. The shock nearly killed her mother."

Natalie put a comforting hand on Mrs. Gerber's forearm. "What a horrible loss. It must have shaken the whole community."

Mrs. Gerber nodded. "It's hard to talk about, even now."

"What about Amara?"

"Never found." Mrs. Gerber sniffed and gave one last swipe at her nose, visibly shaken by the memories. "Still makes me sad. What a waste of two lives."

Natalie stroked the older woman's arm. "What a shock for everyone," she said. An unnecessary death, but seemingly not the one she needed. Pressure locked around her forehead. Watching witnesses grieve over remembered death was one of the hardest parts of the job.

Mrs. Gerber took several steadying breaths. "All in the past. Luckily, my Lily came home, even if somewhat the worse for wear." She was referring to Lily's accident-deformed leg and a scar down the side of her face. "She's home and happy now. Still, would have been better to have the other two come back alive as well."

Nat stroked the older woman's arm. "And no one else went missing?"

"Not on the island. And it was weeks, maybe months, before we started to feel normal and take in the rest of the world. Something could have happened in the meantime." Mrs. Gerber shook her head. "I don't know." Her eyes regained their previous twinkle. "I am eighty-six, you know."

Natalie laughed, set the cups onto the tray and stood. "But your memory is just fine. Thank you. I am sorry they upset you."

"Pshaw. Don't fret yourself. Life is hard sometimes, but no one gets out alive." She chuckled at her own joke and took the tray from Natalie. The two walked to the door and Mrs. G. offered a long, firm hug before Natalie left. Reassurance for both of them.

Down on the walk, Nat turned and looked back. An eighty-six

year old woman replaced the younger looking woman from earlier. *Sorrow ages people.* And looking back triggered tears. Those left behind lived their lives, but sorrow still occupied a corner in their hearts.

Natalie strolled toward her cabin. Who else would be hurt before this case ended? To leave everyone wondering and worrying about the body wasn't right. How could she convince Brayburn to let her continue to the end?

Tomorrow is another day, maybe it will bring more solid information. Am I misjudging Brayburn's intention in sending Curwood to talk to me? Maybe he really is bored. Or maybe I'm tired and paranoid.

Her phone rang, and she hit the Blue-tooth option.

"Parker."

Brayburn. Speak of the devil and he appears.

"Sir?" She turned her back to the ocean breeze.

"Bullpen meeting at ten tomorrow. Be here. Bring whatever you have on your investigation."

"Yes, sir." *Three blind mice, sir. And a pocket full of rye.* Brayburn rang off.

Natalie resumed her walk. *My rhetoric makes no sense, but thinking odd thoughts helps keep a civil tongue in my head.* She let herself into the cabin and collected her overnight things. *But why do those thoughts mainly surface with Brayburn and Curwood?* She'd head for Halifax tonight. *Did my head trauma trigger a dissatisfaction with my life?* With the cabin secured, she got in her car. *Or is it only a mood? One that would have arrived without the explosion.*

****

Natalie woke to a damp Halifax morning with fog obliterating the landscape. *Suits my mood.* She punched the go-button on the coffee and dialed Rob's cell phone. The coffee pot gurgled and the phone gave off ring after ring.

At six rings, Rob answered. "Sorry, just in the, um, I've just finished breakfast at the café. But Turner is watching the site for me."

"Rob, you're allowed a washroom break and food." Nat chuckled. "So what can you tell me so far? I need to be updated for Brayburn's meeting this morning."

"Hang on," Rob said. "Let me get a coffee-to-go and I'll call you back from the car. This place is packed."

"Really, this early on a Saturday, the café is packed?"

"The waitress said there are races today."

"Ah, the junior dory races. I'd forgotten about them. I'll bet there's a large contingent of teenage boys."

"You got it. I've never seen so much postulating. And two guys have major video equipment. Look, I'll call you back."

Natalie poured her own coffee, and taking both phone and full mug with her, entered the extra bedroom in her Halifax apartment. By the time she'd settled in what she called her office, the phone rang.

"Hi, again," Rob said. "First, I need to tell you I called in the Bridgewater detachment last night. I woke when someone tried to get into the trailer. I'd have called you but remembered you were back in Halifax already." *How did he know that? I only told Harvey.*

"What? Did you see who it was?" If they could prove someone was interested in the site, it might give a reason to continue the investigation.

"Maybe. I turned on the light. The rattling stopped. I ran to the door and the far window. There were shadows, but nothing distinct." He paused. "I'd have put it down to the wind, but there were marks around the lock."

"Sounds to me like someone is a little too curious about the findings. Were there any fingerprints?"

"Not a one - not even ours. Obviously wiped clean. They sent out a car from Bridgewater. However, by the time the patrol arrived, whoever fiddled the lock had fled. Constable Conrad said he'd step up the patrols while we're here."

Trust Harvey to be on the ball. "What else have you found?"

"The deceased was young, probably not even twenty. We've cleaned the outside of the skull. There is an obvious indent with cracks radiating out. Hit with something hard, probably blunt and possibly rounded."

"Homicide?"

"Hard to say. She might have been hit, but she also could have fallen against something. The injuries are deep enough to suggest a great deal of force."

"Accidental then?"

"Not my call," Rob said. "Those decisions will be up to you. However, we found bits of decaying fabric under the head. Might have been a pillow. And we found the remains of a watch. I've bagged it and sent it for further examination. I'll send you photos once the watch bits are cleaned up."

"Can you send pictures of the skull now?" Parker asked. "And other new pictures. I have to meet with Brayburn this morning."

"Will do. I'm still cleaning the skull. The orifices are packed with dirt so it is a slow process. And not all the bones are cleaned yet. I'm on it while Karen and the crew start the sifting."

"If you find anything else," Parker said, "please send photos immediately." To wrangle more time, she'd need all the help she could get.

"Can do," Rob said. "And we should be back in the lab tomorrow morning if you want to drop by and have a look at things."

"I'll come by if I can." Natalie thanked Rob and ended the call. The cracked skull, the overnight poking around, both last night and earlier with footsteps at the grave side, should be enough reason to go forward on the investigation. But how would Brayburn see it?

She glanced at the clock. *Time to get moving. I'll know soon enough.*

CHAPTER FIVE

Three hours later Natalie rolled up a ramp onto the highway headed south. The meeting with Brayburn and wading through all the divisional case reports had been like waiting for nail polish to dry--slow and one wrong move would gum things up.

But he'd granted an extension. The attempted interference at the grave weighted her argument, and another case closing left him with two free officers. With no real reasons to deny her, Brayburn reluctantly extended her investigation window. But not by much. She hit the blue-tooth and initiated a call to Harvey.

"We're still in business," she said. "But not for long. We need to make it count. Here's the plan. First, you and me at the old house with luminal and a black light. Photos and samples. Rob confirmed that old blood registers well. If we find any, we'll turn it over to him."

She passed two cars and eased off the gas. "Next, we'll cover the entire province and go wider with the computer search for missing persons. Mrs. Gerber said hippies came to the island. They could have come from anywhere and maybe one of them didn't make it home. I'll get Devon to do the searches."

"You really plan to hit the ground running, don't you?" Harvey said. "I'll get the gear and meet you at the old house."

"I'll call Devon," Natalie said. "And I need a quick visit with Adam. See you soon."

But the distance demanded time even if she wanted to go faster. On the road, she called Devon. "Hey, you have the Lexus-Nexus program, and Greg said to use it. There are some key search words on the desk. You may think of others. You're clear on what we're looking for?"

"Couldn't be clearer," Devon said. "I'm on it, boss."

Natalie jerked back. Was she coming on too strong? Turning into Brayburn wasn't on the agenda. "Sorry, I'm a bit keyed up."

Devon laughed. "It's fine. Go on."

She reached the grocery store and found Adam and Mutt in the backyard. "How's it going?" she asked.

"Good." He put down his bottle of juice. "Really good. I found two dollars and ninety cents down at the beach this morning."

"Ah hum. The metal detector." A thought trickled across her mind. "The word is getting out about what Mutt found," she added. "You can talk about it now."

"Sweet!" He air-punched with one hand. "And can I go look at the site?"

She paused over the question. "Well. You could skirt the area. You know, go around the edges. But stay well back from the yellow tape and don't go near the house. And you'll have to wait until I can go with you."

He nodded. "I understand. We can't contaminate the scene."

Natalie ran a hand over her mouth to hide the smile sneaking onto her lips. *An old man in a boy's body.* She stood. "Take care," she said. "I'll see you later. I have to go now."

"Investigating, eh?"

She smiled again, not hiding it this time. "Always."

"I'll walk out with you," Adam said and picked up his empty juice container and the metal detector. "I'll do practice sweeping around the yard, so I'll be ready."

"Good plan," Natalie said. "See you, probably tomorrow. Okay."

"Sure." Adam walked her to her car and turned and ran off. *What a kid.*

Natalie headed to the estate's parking area. Going up the hill and through the woods took no more time than hiking in from Westerly Road. She dropped her overnight bag in Cabin Three, grabbed her flashlight and ran out the door. Pushing through the shrubbery at the top of the hill, she halted where Harvey waited.

He was lounging in his habitual pose of arms and ankles crossed, back against the house and toothpick in the corner of his mouth. He pushed away and stood firmly on both feet, removing the toothpick as he did so. The toothpick disappeared into his shirt pocket.

I wonder if he ever throws them away, or if it's some self-renewing pick.

"About time," he said and gave her a hug. "Now let's see what's inside."

****

Harvey hefted his flashlight and led the way to the door facing the ocean. It squealed but gave under his push. If it had ever been locked, the lock had long since given up functioning. Inside, air left behind and turned dry and dusty washed over him. *Whew. Stale.* Behind him, Nat coughed.

Light filtered in the open door. And joined sunlight sneaking through the boards on the window. Dust motes, disturbed by air currents and their footsteps, floated around them. He switched on the flashlight and illuminated the abandoned room. *Dusty, creepy, and forlorn.*

A kitchen with eating area ran the depth of the house. Dust-covered lino, lay littered with twigs and leaves, probably dragged in by mice.

"I wonder when anyone visited this place last." He turned a full 360 degrees in the middle of the room. "If the teens came here years ago, there may have been others since." An old sofa, leaking stuffing, crouched forlornly under the window. On the left, an old round-cornered refrigerator hunkered with its door hanging open. Beside it, a big wooden box crumbled, its sides caved in. The stove, a monstrosity from the past, loomed in the alcove beyond.

"Wow. Now, there is a stove," Nat said.

Harvey inspected it and lifted a round lid on the top. "Looks like a combination wood burner and," he said, checking the second lid, "maybe stove oil. I've never seen anything like it." He extended his inspection. "The cupboards are empty. Everything cleared out except dust."

At the far end of the room, he swung open a door. *Everything in this place sags, even the mood.* A foyer footed a staircase and offered access to a second room and the solid front door.

Nat pointed to a small window over the door. "That's a transom window, isn't it?" Fractured light slanted through the grubby glass. "This place is seriously eerie."

Harvey shifted his light up the narrow, solid-walled staircase. "We haven't fallen through the floor and the ceiling hasn't collapsed. We might as well continue." He started up, avoiding mouse droppings on the stair treads. The steps ended at another square landing. As below, doors on the landing opened to rooms on either side. Straight ahead a third door hung on aging hinges.

Nat pushed it open, and Harvey looked over her shoulder. A narrow bathroom with a shower stall occupied the space. Cabinets covered every wall. Dead flies littered the sink and shower. Spider webs connected the shower door to the stall itself, and brown stains marked where water at one time occupied the toilet bowl. Nat turned and a spider web draped her face. She shuddered and, clawing at the web with both hands, bumped up against Harvey.

He steadied her, held her against himself. "Take it easy."

She rubbed her face on his shirt, erasing the final remnants of the spider web. "You get a web in the face and see how easy you take it." She stepped past him and faced another door.

The dim room held only litter. The boards over the dormer window cast dark shadows. Harvey peered out between the boards. "This is over the veranda. I can see the fallen tree off to the right."

Extra sunlight sneaked into the second room where one of the boards on the dormer hung by a nail. Three candle stubs sat on their respective bottle lids laced with webs and dead flies. A box in the corner appeared to have served as a garbage receptacle. Nothing but the sad remnants of someone's party.

Harvey stood on the small landing and stared down the steps.

Natalie joined him. "The place is a perfect site for a murder," she said, and shivered "I can feel the evil or the sadness in the place. It's like a cloak around my shoulders."

Harvey put an arm around her. "No worries, I'll save you from the ghosts."

"Thanks," she said, "just how do you plan to do that? Ghosts are sneaky, you know."

He laughed and reached for a toothpick.

"Okay," Nat said. "What hit Jane Doe's head?"

"Nothing applicable up here," he said. "I'd say the kitchen is the best bet. Stove, wood box and cabinets all have edges."

"I agree," Nat said and started down the stairs. "Let's start there."

In the kitchen, Harvey retrieved the gear from its case, adjusted the camera settings, and photographed the entire room, including close-ups of any edges. "Let's start the luminal at the stove," he said and letting the camera hang around his neck, picked up the black light. Turning off the flashlight, he allowed the darkness to settle around them. "Okay, hit it, Nat."

Nat stood dead center in front of the stove and sprayed lines of luminal evenly across its surface. Harvey operated the black light, but found nothing in that first patch.

"At least we know the surface isn't splattered with blood," he said, and pointed along the front trim with its rounded metal, top edge. "Try there."

With a steady hand, she sprayed down the right side and across the front edge. Harvey followed with the black light.

At the front left their efforts paid off. Blue streaks decorated the chrome corner. "Bingo," Harvey said and snapped close-up pictures before stepping back to get mid-range and wide shots. The thirty seconds before the Luminal faded wasn't a long time. "Got them all," he said.

"Blood," Nat said. "Rob wasn't kidding when he said old blood would still show. Conclusions? Suggestions?"

"If she hit her head on the corner, she could have fallen to the floor. Especially if she'd been pushed."

Nat sprayed luminal evenly over the floor, coating back along the side and across the front of the stove. Harvey's light revealed additional blue speckles and pools.

"Keep working out," he directed, "until we stop getting a reaction." He handed off the light and snapped pictures in rapid succession. The blue lit area ended leaving a rough circle centered on a spot about a foot from the stove.

"Well," Nat said, "this might be our crime scene. She would have hit there," she said, pointing at the stove, "and fallen so that her head ended here. "But," she said, raising one finger, "we can't be sure, although it's unlikely, someone might have dropped steaks before cooking them. Time will tell if our blood residue is human or not. It is, however, enough to get the crime scene gurus to do this right." She pulled out her phone, switching it to speaker mode.

"Dr. Zhang," she said, "we have a possible crime scene." She described their findings. "When can someone get here to gather evidence? And process the place?"

"Hang on a minute," Zhang said and put Nat on hold. Time ticked by before she returned. "Rob says he'll be there right after supper. He's willing to put in extra time."

"Send battery operated lights," Nat said. "There's no power."

Harvey leaned closer. "We're going to put locks on the doors. Have him call one of us when he's close."

Nat disconnected. "Great, task number one completed. Let's lock this place down and check on Devon and see where to go next."

Harvey watched the excitement dance across her face. Although she'd questioned going back into the field, she loved being there, loved investigating. "Get a move on then," he said, "there is more information to find."

Outside he dug out locks, clasps, and a drill. He installed the clasps and managed to get the doors secured. Nat unrolled and fastened yellow tape across them. "I'll do the front," he said and taking the box and its gear headed around the house. After repeating the same process, he returned to find Natalie viewing pictures on the camera.

"Everything secured," he said. "How did the photos turn out?"

"They'll do the job," she said. "There's no doubt we've uncovered blood."

Harvey closed up the tool box and straightened to answer his phone. "Conrad?" the voice on the other end said, "Rob here, we found a clue to Miss Doe's identity."

Harvey turned on the speaker mode. "Go ahead, Rob."

"Our lady wore a silver necklace with a half-heart pendant. I found it embedded in the dirt in her chest cavity."

Jewelry. Someone might know it, maybe even gave it to her. Excitement, probably matching Nat's, surged through him. Solid clues did it for him every time.

"Excellent. Is there an inscription?"

"Nothing personal," Rob said. "The word 'ends' and 'ever' are inscribed on it."

"Thanks for letting us know so promptly," Harvey said. "Send me the pictures."

"Will do. And I'll meet you about seven at the house, if that works at your end?"

"Good enough. See you then." Harvey pocketed the phone. "At last, two items to show people. Come on, let's tell Devon. Maybe there was a necklace mentioned in one of the missing persons reports." Harvey gave Nat a quick hug and a peck on the cheek.

"Hey, we're on the job here. Stay focused."

"There's no one around - and a quick hug after getting good news is acceptable." He winked and took her chin in his hand. "I can do better." He lowered his mouth toward hers.

Nat sighed and swatted his arm. "Cut it out. We have a case to solve."

His laugh followed her as she stomped off. One of these days she'd stop being so up-tight about their relationship.

The Caleb Cove Security offices, with a live computer screen and strewn paper on the desk, stood ready but vacant.

Nat stopped in the office doorway. "Hey, Devon," she called.

"Right here." Devon entered from the main house carrying cookies.

Harvey inhaled. "Are those Vie's ginger snaps?" The problem with the cookies became clear. Everyone made them. Everyone served them. Everyone ate them, and no doubt, everyone including him, was putting on weight.

"Yup." Devon held the plate toward him, and he took two. "And the coffee in the pot is fresh. I knew there'd be brainstorming to do and figured sustenance would be needed."

Harvey headed for the coffee station. "One for you, ladies?"

He got the expected answer and joined them with three mugs of coffee. "Here you go. Caffeine to set your brains on alert." He rolled a chair over to the computer. With the coffee, he ate two more cookies. *I'll worry about weight when this case is over.*

****

Natalie stared at Devon's paper stack. The woman had certainly had a productive search volume-wise.

"Here," Devon said and handed printed pages to Natalie.

"These are the articles on the two girls who drowned in 1969. Gloria Roberts and Amara Krause." She turned back to the desk. "The same summer, there were a few missing girls reported in Nova Scotia, but three came back and one was found dead. All accounted for."

Crackles assaulted Natalie's temples and lodged behind her eyes. *Another dead girl.* She inhaled the aroma and slugged back coffee.

Devon handed other pages to Harvey. "However, it might be worth finding out who the dead girl was with. I did include the other Atlantic Provinces in the search but haven't read through what came up."

"Useful progress." Natalie scanned the first article and handed it over to Harvey. "If you can track down the other hippies, we might unearth useful information." Her phone chimed, and the necklace photos popped up in a text. She sent them to the printer.

Natalie waited, her eyes closed and her brain tuned to the whirring of the machine. *Focus. Don't let the static win.* She added note cards with new information. There were moments when old-school pen and paper triggered more than computer lists. And the chunks of data could be more easily arranged when on the cards. "The other photos and materials are in the war room. Let's get these posted."

In the other room, Natalie stood with new cards and photos in hand. She pointed to the items already posted. "Our list starts with Mutt finding the partial appendage and ends with the grave. Now we need all the information between finding the grave and now."

One by one she stuck new cards on the board. "Here are our confirmations so far. The skeleton is female, late teens. Most likely cause of death, the blow to the head." She tapped the cards and continued posting others in chronological order naming the information as she went.

She added a card for Gloria and Amara in a separate side panel. "They left around the same time and maybe there are events that overlapped with their story."

Harvey pinned pictures of the full skeleton, the close-ups of the skull and the first-found hand down the left of the board. "Rob took a slice of the tree trunk and dated it at forty to fifty years for starters," he said. "But telling the age of a tree by the rings isn't as exact as the popular view would have it."

Natalie posted the necklace pictures last. "Take a good look at these. They are our most concrete lead to date." She stepped away and viewed the board as a whole. Unease prickled her hairline. *What am I missing?* No answer came but the pulsing demanded an adjustment to the board. She stepped forward and corrected the alignment of the top row of cards, making sure they were even. *Much better.* But the missing detail still eluded her.

She turned her back on the board. Maybe her ears would work better. She sipped coffee. "Okay, folks. Thoughts?"

Harvey tilted in the wheeled office chair and drummed his fingers. "Although we haven't found any evidence to prove it," he said, "my gut says she has a connection to the Cove. I'm not into the hippie angle."

"I agree with Harvey on one point," Devon said. "She came here alive. The bridges weren't built until nineteen seventy-eight. It's not likely someone would bring a body over here to bury it. If she came from the mainland, she arrived alive."

"Perhaps there was an altercation between the locals and the hippies and it ended badly." Harvey tilted forward and propped his elbows on his knees.

Natalie handed her camera to Devon. "True, especially seeing we did find a potential murder site. We need a set of the recent photos for ourselves and to send to FIS."

She found a marker and added a question mark and 'locals or summer people' on the board. "Maybe we can't track hippie campers, but we can find out which property owners were at their summer places in August."

"Properties have changed hands in the few last decades," Harvey said. "But there will be records to trace the previous owners if we can fit in all the phone calls. We really need to narrow down the time frame."

"Whoever killed her, knew her," Nat said. "The fabric under her head suggested a pillow. A stranger wouldn't bother."

Devon returned from the printer. "I always wonder what good a pillow does a corpse."

"There may have been blood on the pillow," Harvey said. "If it was accidental he, or she, might have put the pillow under the victim's head hoping she wasn't dead. And then they buried it to hide evidence. Although the placement under the head is telling. It could have been tossed into the grave anywhere."

Nat rubbed her temples and rolled her shoulders. *Back down. I don't have time for a headache.* "Local kids used the place as a hideout, and meet-up spot. She might have been there for a romantic hook-up. Maybe we have a male killer."

Harvey stood. "If two people were romantically involved, I'd go for an argument ending in a shoving match. One resulting with the girl falling against the stove." He placed his hands on Natalie's shoulders and massaged with his thumbs.

Natalie tipped her head. "Thanks, Harvey. Feels better."

Devon perched on her chair. "But if accidental, why bury her and not report it?"

"Panic?" Natalie offered.

"A lot to lose if the cause of death became public?" Harvey's contribution.

Devon added, "An unwanted pregnancy, and the father flipped out?"

"I'll ask the M.E. But I don't think they can tell unless she was more than three months pregnant. Before that the baby's bones wouldn't have formed enough to last."

"The killer may have forced himself on her, and she tried to get away," Devon said.

"If so, he definitely wouldn't want anyone to know." Harvey's comment brought the discussion skidding to an end.

"Any or several of our ideas may be true." Natalie paced to the counter along the wall and turning, leaned against it. "Let's look at what we might find and what we need to ask. They are doing DNA testing and hope to get a match between the skeletal remains and the blood found on the stove and floor in the kitchen. The samples are old material, but they'll try."

Harvey added a card with 'DNA and blood' on it and joined it by an arrow to the body.

Devon stood. "Printer's done. I'll get those shots from the house."

She returned with photos and handed them to Harvey. He placed the ones with the blue luminal on the board and joined them to the skeleton with a question mark.

Natalie massaged her forehead and ignored the thumping in her head. "If it's human blood I'd say we can assume that's the crime scene in the kitchen. If they can get DNA we may find out who she is."

"Do we have a narrower time window yet?" Devon asked. "Even pinpointing a specific year would be a start."

Harvey pointed at the tree trunk card. "So far, all we know is the forty to fifty years. Or sometime in the late sixties or early seventies."

"The one new piece of information is the silver necklace Rob found. This charm." Natalie tapped the photo. "Is only half a heart. There would have been a matching half." *Hearts given with love or friendship, signifying a close bond between two people. What went wrong?* "If we find the owner of the matching half, we'll have a solid lead to at least information."

"Perhaps it came from the killer and is long gone," Devon added. "And guys don't go for hearts on chains, so it might have been a female."

"If it was around her neck, it might have been hidden under her top." Natalie put a hand to her own chest where her special necklace rested out of the sight of public eyes.

Harvey winked at her. "Do you think she was two-timing the guy? And the chain and charm came from another boyfriend? If he figured it out, he might have flipped out?"

Natalie laughed. "You have experience, do you, Harvey?"

He didn't answer her question. "When you're young and in love, it could trigger an angry reaction."

"Another possibility," she agreed. She stood back and looked at all the pictures again. "We'll have to roll with what we have. Timing, necklace, the girl's age. It's not much, but it is better than nothing."

Devon pointed to the back of the medallion. "But what do 'ends' and 'ever' mean?"

"My guess," Natalie said, "is 'friends forever.' Now they'd say BFFs but I think that term came along much later." She tapped the file box. "Meanwhile, the official reports we've collected are in here. When we get a minute, we can all read them again and become familiar with the small details. Often a case is cracked by noting a fluke around an insignificant detail. And Devon, please continue with what you can find on the computer."

"I'm on it." Devon disappeared into the office.

Harvey groaned. "And once we narrow the date, we need to track down residents and summer people."

"Do you think we can conscript Turner?" Natalie asked. "We have a lot to cover."

"Sure, after all, I am the local lead on the case," Harvey said. "I'll put him on stand-by." He dialed his phone and walked to the main room.

Left alone with the meager evidence, Natalie pushed back her hair and held it. With the time that had passed, and the convoluted movement of potential witnesses, it seemed an unlikely case to solve. She rolled her head forward, stretching tense neck muscles. Her biggest stumbling block would be time or lack of it. What year did the girl die? The tree trunk suggested about fifty years. But with no missing person to check against, even that necklace wasn't much of a help.

In spite of the stumbling blocks, they had a chance. *And a tough case with a chance is right up my alley. Have to admit I'm having a weird type of fun.*

CHAPTER SIX

Harvey strolled back to the war room. At the door he paused. Nat stood rubbing the back of her neck but with a smile hovering on her face. *She's fighting a headache but loving the job.*

Easing in behind her, he gently removed her hands. "Let me help," he said and took over the task. "Just wondering," he said. "Are you liking being back on an active case?"

She exhaled noisily. "Harvey, your hands are amazing. You can give a back rub with the best of them. And yes, my brain is loving the questions, the searching and the potential to solve a murder."

He nodded even though she couldn't see him. He'd known getting back on the horse would be good for her. He applied pressure on two tight knots and felt them ease. Nat moaned and leaned back against him.

"I could do without the tense muscles though." She stepped away and turned to smile at him. "Good think you have my back."

As usual, curls swept against her face. He brushed one of them back. "We can't have you imploding, can we?" She flicked her fingers against his chest. "Come on, Harvey, once more around the mulberry bush. There are people who were here back in the day. Time to talk to them again now that we have more information."

Harvey held her hand on the way to the car and opened the passenger door. "In you get."

Mrs. Gerber's place was closest and on the way to the Cove. He pulled into her yard minutes later. Nat went to the door and knocked. Harvey leaned against the car, watching.

Mrs. Gerber opened the door. "Officer Parker?"

"Sorry to bother you," Nat said. "I need a few minutes, if you don't mind."

"Always ready to talk," Mrs. G. said and opened the door.

"No thanks, I'll only be a few minutes." Natalie said. "You mentioned hippies on the island. In 1969? Correct?"

"Yes. The year Lily took off."

"Did hippies come here often?"

Mrs. G. shook her head. "For some reason 1969 attracted beach parties and camping. Like I said the other day, they all came in August and they all left after the Labor Day weekend. They were in the store a lot, buying milk and bread and sometimes peanut butter. They must have lived on sandwiches."

Harvey, hearing her comment, shifted his toothpick from left to right. *1969, the summer of sex, drugs and rock and roll—a recipe for trouble.* Looked like they could assume the body came from August 1969. *Gives us the starting point we need.* Crossing his ankles, he waited while Nat finished questioning Mrs. Gerber.

Nat produced the photo. "Do you recognize this necklace?"

Mrs. G. picked her glasses off her ample bosom and, with the chain dangling, held them to her eyes. She turned the photo several ways, peering through glasses. "No, I don't remember ever seeing that one." She handed back the picture. "Did it come from the grave?"

Nat tucked the picture back in her folder. "Yes."

The old lady shook her head. "So sad, all those young people so full of life. What a way for one of them to end up."

"True, Mrs. G., so true. Thanks for your help." Nat turned and jumped the three steps to the walk. The screen door clicked closed, and the old woman watched her go.

Nat took a double step as if the walk eluded her, and Harvey came to attention. *She's not as steady as she'd like me to believe. Has she been taking her meds? I bet not.* But she caught herself and continued toward him.

He opened the passenger door for her. "Who next?" he asked.

"Lem and Lenya, I think," she said. "They were teenagers that summer. Lenya first. Teenage girls notice jewelry. Mrs. Gerber also said hippies stayed at the campground. Two good reasons to talk to her." Nat rested her head on the headrest.

Harvey shot a quick look in her direction. *She's still fighting a headache. We need to get today wrapped up and get her off her feet.*

****

Campers lined up at the red A-frame office, delaying progress. Natalie rolled down her window and breathed in the sea breeze. *Take the chance to relax. The skeleton has been a secret for fifty years or so, it can wait an extra fifteen minutes.*

Harvey stretched his arm over and, sliding his hand under her neck, squeezed gently. She welcomed his massaging touch. *He knows I'm going down for the count. Good thing he's got my back, in case worst comes to worst.*

After the last camper headed for the camping sites, the sign over the door switched to *No Vacancy*. Harvey pulled into the parking area beside the front step. He joined Natalie and put an arm around her back, ushering her up the steps and through the door. A bell announced their arrival, and Lenya looked up from filing registration cards.

"Natalie. Harvey. How are you?" Abandoning the filing, she came forward to hug them. "I hear you have a case. This island certainly keeps the police in business."

Natalie returned the hug and stepped back. "Must be the curse, although your aunt says it doesn't exist." They both laughed.

Harvey tipped his head and pursed his lips. "Don't let Lem hear you speak against ghosts. He says curses and ghosts are good for business."

Lenya grinned. "I'll remember. What can I do for you today?" She indicated the canteen. "Tea? Some chocolate?"

Natalie held up her hand. "Please, no more tea. My hind teeth are already floating."

Lenya pressed her lips together and looked at Natalie sideways. "Around here we always combine tea and talk." She clutched both hands against her solar plexus. "Don't know if we dare break the tradition." She held the pose for about two seconds and then burst out laughing.

Harvey and Natalie laughed, enjoying her joke.

Natalie headed to the candy rack. "I wouldn't turn down chocolate though."

"Chocolate is second best to tea," Lenya said, waving her hand toward the array of candy. "Pick your poison, and let's go into the office. The chairs are more comfortable than the stools."

Natalie grabbed an *Oh Henry. Maybe chocolate will settle my head.*

Harvey scooped up a *Coffee Crisp* and they followed Lenya to the office. Nice to have privacy, in case someone ignored the *No Vacancy* sign. Natalie eyed the two leather recliners facing the desk. "You don't skimp on comfort, do you?"

"I spend so much time in this place, I need a comfortable retreat right in the building." Lenya reached down and pulled a lever raising a foot rest. "My legs and feet appreciate the elevation. There's one on your chair as well."

Nat glanced at the lever but didn't activate the foot rest. "What did you hear about the current case?" Without a doubt, Lenya knew something. As a main link in the island information tree, she always did. *Probably has the strongest case of osmosis powers too, other than Lem.*

"Not much. You have a rough grave by the old house and a skeleton." She sighed. "I remember going there as a kid. We loved to play away from our parents' prying eyes. They probably would have had a heart attack if they'd seen us sitting up on the roof of the main veranda."

"Who made up the group?"

"Goodness. Lem and Lily and Phil, when he visited his uncle. And kids from the summer places. I remember sitting in the darkened kitchen and telling scary stories. More than once we ran screaming away from the building thanks to some creak or crack in the old place."

Harvey tapped his pen. "Is that the Phil Doucette we locked up a couple of years ago?"

"One and the same." Lenya's eyes lost their focus. "Older kids went as well, but not at the same time. They were allowed out in the evening, and I'm sure they hung out there whenever rain made a beach party impossible. Some came across in motor boats from Second Island."

Her information tallied with Mrs. Gerber's story and Curwood's information from day one. "When did kids stop going there?"

"I'm not sure. I think we were the last generation. When our kids came along, the trees had grown and boxed it in and we certainly didn't tell them." She chuckled. "As adults, we didn't think it was safe." Blinking, she returned to the present. "When do you think the body was buried? Was it there all the time and we didn't know?"

Harvey cleared his throat. "The M.E. thinks about forty to fifty years ago."

Lenya's head pulled back. "Good heavens, that's when we were there. Maybe there was a reason to be frightened and run screaming. Who do you think it is?"

"That's what we're trying to figure out," Natalie said. "There was no identification in the grave." *So little information. Another nail in my headache.* "Your aunt can't remember anyone going missing permanently. We're searching police reports and newspapers from the mainland to see if anyone else reported a girl in her late teens as missing."

"Late teens? The poor girl. All those years buried." Lenya's voice trembled. "How did she die?"

Harvey spoke up. "A blow to the head most likely."

Lenya's face paled. "Killed, as in murdered?"

Natalie threw in the official statement. "Details have not been determined. It might have been an accident."

Silence settled around them. Lenya's face paled and she trembled. "It must be terrible for her family," she said. "I know how hard it is. I lost my sister." She stopped and cleared her throat. "After they found Gloria's body washed up on shore, they assumed Amara drowned, too. For years, I thought them wrong, that she'd show up, just come home one day." She sighed. "Eventually, I had to accept the official decision about her death."

She turned back to Nat. "Will you be able to find out who the poor girl is?"

"We're doing what we can. We've been told August 1969 saw quite a few hippies on the island. Both at the campground and also squatting on other sites. Do you remember?"

Lenya grinned. "Oh ya. Fascinating. All that long hair on the guys and long, flowing dresses on the girls."

"So the girls all wore dresses?" If so the denim scrap with the body might rule out the hippies.

"Pretty much. Although some wore jeans and flowered tops—those cropped ones." She ran a flat hand across her rib cage.

Natalie allowed herself a small sigh. "Our Miss Doe wore jewelry. We hope someone will come forward and identify it."

Lenya laughed and color returned to her cheeks. "That might be tricky. The campers all wore long necklaces with beads and flowers. Even the guys."

"Rob found one with the body, but it's a different style. Here, I have a picture." Natalie dug it out. "You might remember it." She passed over the photo.

The close up showed the long chain and the jagged half-heart clearly. Like her aunt, Lenya held the photo at an angle to catch the light.

"Oh." Lenya gasped.

"You recognize it?"

"Yes. No. I don't know. It can't be." Lenya closed her eyes and shook her head several times. She opened her eyes and looked again. Her whisper slid out. "It can't be."

Natalie froze. If Lenya recognized the necklace, it could be both good and bad. Good if it gave them a lead. Bad it if led to someone she knew. She shifted, sliding forward on her seat and putting a hand on Lenya's arm. "Why do you think you might recognize this?"

"Gloria and Amara wore necklaces like this. One-half of the heart each. And the backs, when they held them together, said 'Friends Forever.'"

Nat sighed inwardly. *So I guessed correctly, the inscription is part of Friends Forever.*

Natalie sensed the confusion radiating from Lenya.

"The one like this, the right side, belonged to Gloria." Lenya's hand shook, rattling the photo. "What's...," She drew in a sharp breath. "Is there anything on the back of this?" She held the photo out in one hand.

Natalie took the photo. "I'm sorry. "'Ever and ends' are inscribed on the back of this one."

Lenya stood and turned away, her head down.

Natalie waited.

Lenya turned back to face them. Her arms were straight and

her fists pressed against her sides. "Not possible. No way would Gloria have given this to anyone. This one is not hers." Her jaw muscle twitched. "It was a fad and lots of girls had them."

"Possibly," Harvey said, his voice low. "However, how many of those other girls were here on the island?"

"Oh. Oh." Lenya sank down on the chair. She perched on the edge sideways and one hand gripped the chair arm. Her breath rasped. "I don't understand. IF the body you found is Gloria? Who did we bury in the graveyard?"

Natalie put her items back in the briefcase. Who was in the graveyard indeed? And who killed Gloria and buried her by the old house? And what happened to Lenya's sister, Amara? Questions begetting questions.

Oh, blue ducks and little puddles. The ramifications will rip through the community, the police force and the memories of two girls. And the killer? What happened to them? What have they been doing for all the years since? *Are they even still alive?*

Harvey, looking disconcerted, handed Natalie a tissue box. She passed it to the sobbing woman. The sorrow and tension in the room settled around Natalie, merging with the light flashes behind her eyes. The aura rippling in her vision field increased, and the migraine settled in to stay. She put her hands over her face.

A hand settled on her shoulder. *Harvey.* He knew the signs. He'd help her. His voice faded in and out along with Lenya's responses.

"I'll take Natalie to the car," he said. "And I'll be back. You've had a nasty shock. Who should I call to come and stay with you?"

"Lily, call Lily. But don't let her tell her mother. Maybe we're wrong." The doubt in Lenya's voice stabbed sharply against the lack of doubt in Natalie's head.

How could they misidentify a body and bury it under the wrong name?

She stood and staring straight ahead, managed to stay focused until he helped her into the passenger seat. Harvey fastened her seatbelt and headed back inside. She closed her eyes and counted her breaths. She barely managed to stay upright.

CHAPTER SEVEN

Natalie opened her eyes to light spilling in around the bedroom blinds. She rolled over. *I'm dressed.* She adjusted her covers. *And this is a quilt only. The clock reads seven thirty. But is it evening or morning. Damn migraine.*

She dragged out of bed and padded to the bathroom. Morning duties handled, she headed for the kitchen. Harvey sat at the breakfast bar sipping coffee. That didn't help settle the time. He always drank coffee.

"Good morning," he said. "How are you feeling today?"

At least his greeting settled the time. "I'm fine?"

He raised an eyebrow. "You don't sound sure."

"Leave it alone. I am fine. I'll be fine. Now, where's the coffee?"

"Relax, Miss Grumpy Pants. Keep your shirt on." Harvey brought her a coffee.

Hoisting her rear end onto the stool, she slid until she was sitting solidly with her elbows on the counter. She accepted the coffee and wrapped her hands around the mug. "Ah, the elixir of a clear head."

Harvey retrieved his own coffee. "Let me know when you have a civil tongue in your head." The kiss he planted on her forehead softened his words.

She drank three long sips. "Okay, I'm ready. What happened after we left the campground? I have no recollection."

"I'm not surprised. You had a headache that cut you off from the world. I got you here, tipped you into bed, and made you take a pill."

Natalie held her head in her hands. "Lovely, just lovely." She dropped one hand and peered sideways at him. "Who saw me?"

"Only Lenya." He paused. "Do you remember what she told us yesterday?"

Natalie lifted her head from her hands. "Yes, I remember the necklace story. My head exploded shortly after." She groaned. "This really complicates things. I suppose I need to talk to Brayburn. Did I miss anything I need to know?"

"Only the usual. I'm sure you could guess." He ticked off items on his fingers.

"I asked Lenya to search for identifying pictures and information about Gloria. She'll bring them here this morning.

"I tracked down Gloria's mother. She's still alive and living in a senior's community in Halifax. I asked her to cooperate for a DNA sample and she will.

"And I let Devon know there's a high likelihood the body is Gloria Roberts. She's adjusting her searches."

He closed his fingers. "Once you've talked to Brayburn, we can arrange for FIS to get that DNA sample."

"What would I do without you?" Nat leaned over and rested her head against Harvey's shoulder.

"I'm sure you'd manage," he replied dryly, "but it wouldn't be as much fun. By the way, my staying here may attract some attention. Even if I'm in the spare bedroom, Brayburn might not like it."

"To heck with Brayburn," Nat said, "and the horse he rode in on." She drained the coffee mug and found her phone. "It's eight. He'll be in his office." She dialed. He answered.

"Boss, we have a good news, bad news scenario here. Which do you want first?"

"Whatever is most logical?"

None of it is logical.

She outlined Lenya's reaction to the necklace photo. "It's quite likely our remains are Gloria Roberts." She drew a deep breath.

Brayburn jumped into the gap. "And the bad news?"

"Everyone here is under the assumption they buried Gloria Roberts in the local graveyard years ago."

"What the hell?"

"Here's the short version." She filled him in on the runaway theory and the supposed drowning. "Therefore, there are questions.

If the skeleton is Gloria Roberts who is the body in the graveyard? And how did Gloria end up dead and buried at the old house? And where is her best friend who, by all accounts, never left her side? And how the heck did the other body get identified as Gloria?"

"You've certainly dug up a fine mess. Do you have a plan to deal with it? "Brayburn's voice suggested it was her fault.

"We've found Gloria's mother living in Halifax. I'll ask FIS to get a sample for a DNA match. If our Jane Doe is Gloria, we'll look for her friend's body. And we'll start finding everyone who even sneezed in the Cove that week. The body they buried as Gloria can wait."

Brayburn grunted. "Make it work, and work fast. Hear me?"

"Yes, sir." Natalie continued. "Once we unravel the details, we may face an exhumation and a wider search regarding the already buried body."

Brayburn's curse exploded through the phone. When not happy with the progression of a case, he wasn't shy about letting his displeasure show.

Natalie waited. After his outburst, it was the only sane thing to do.

Brayburn's breath huffed through the phone. "Now, don't take this the wrong way, Constable, but are you up to handling this muddle?"

"Yes. I can handle it."

Another grunt. *The man needs a new reaction.*

"And you're not experiencing any relapses, no flashbacks, or anxiety attacks?"

She crossed her fingers. "No, none of those." After all, he didn't specify headaches.

"Well, I suppose I have to let you carry on." *He sounds disappointed.* "But if you need help with interviews or following up, let me know."

"Certainly. At the moment, Constable Conrad is working closely with me." She crossed her fingers again. "And Curwood is still down here on vacation, as far as I know. We can use him as a sounding board if need be." She glanced at the clock. Not even nine in the morning and she'd told two fabrications already. *Self-preservation.*

"Keep me up to date." And Brayburn was gone.

"Typical." She growled at the phone. "Bossy."

Harvey leaned in, his voice suggestive. "Working closely with Constable Conrad are you?"

Natalie patted his cheek. "Down boy." She slid off the stool. "We need to call Dr. Zhang or Rob, but first I need food." She found rice cereal and retrieved the milk from the fridge. "If we go on the assumption we've found Gloria Roberts, we can build a timeline for the day the girls were last seen."

Harvey picked up his phone. "I'll call Rob. Eat—you need nourishment."

She shoveled in cereal and washed it down with coffee. *Food helps. I feel better.*

"Rob says they're backed up now with current investigations, but they can fit in a DNA sample from Mrs. Roberts. However, searching for another buried body is a time consumer. He'll put it on the board and see what they can do. But it won't be in the next few days for sure."

Natalie took her dish to the sink. "So, while we wait, we talk to people. Let's find out what all went on around here in August 1969."

Harvey pulled out his notepad. "We need to find out who decided the body they buried is Gloria Roberts." Out came the ubiquitous toothpick. "But, in the sixties, they didn't have the forensics we have. Making a mistake could have been *dead* easy depending on the body's decomposition." He waggled his eyebrows.

Natalie groaned. "Too early for puns, Harvey."

He grinned. "There will be case files though. I'll get Turner to track them down."

"Good. Now I need a shower and fresh clothing before Lenya shows up. Keep yourself busy." She exited the kitchen and closing the bedroom door behind her, started peeling off clothing. *After sleeping fully dressed, a shower is going to feel fantastic.*

****

Harvey flipped through news bulletins on his phone. The running water beat against his awareness. She'd slept like the dead, but her pale complexion revealed lingering stress. *Not good for an officer in the middle of an investigation.*

Her door opened and she crossed the room toward him. He looked up and smiled. "You look more alive."

"Thanks. My migraine left me with a hangover." She greeted him with a kiss. "More coffee should clear the final fuzz in my head though."

Harvey obliged. "Here, sit on the sofa and relax." He handed over the mug. But looking at her wan face and pale complexion, he wasn't sure coffee would do the job.

Half hiding behind his own mug, he kept an eye on Nat as she settled and cradled the mug before downing several sips. The lines in her forehead relaxed and she sighed.

Maybe the coffee will work. Harvey plunked down on the other end of the sofa. "How many migraines have plagued you recently?"

She put out her palm in a 'who-me' gesture.

Harvey turned in his seat, facing her. "Natalie Ann." He sounded like an inquiring parent and softened his voice. "Are you taking your meds?" As much as he knew he wasn't her keeper, he needed to keep them both safe. To do otherwise would be irresponsible. Never mind his personal interest in keeping her healthy.

Nat blatantly avoided him. "This is the only one I've had in three months," she said. "Honest."

She wasn't getting away with a partial answer. "And the meds?"

Resting the coffee on her leg, Nat ran a finger up and down the mug. "Maybe I missed a few doses."

Harvey stretched his arm along the sofa back and tapped her shoulder with one finger. "And didn't the lack of migraines help get you back into field work? If you have another, you need to put yourself back in the office." He slid his hand to her neck and massaged. "If you'd been alone, it could have turned out badly."

In the end, she looked over and grinned. "Sure, Dad, sure." She stuck out her tongue.

Harvey glared. "Don't joke. Promise me you'll take this seriously?"

Nat tipped her head against his wrist. "Yes, I know. You're right. I can't risk putting anyone else in danger."

He cupped her cheek. "I'm more worried about you being in danger. After recovering from what you've been through, it'd be a shame to die because of a headache."

A knock at the door cut short the discussion.

He dropped a kiss on Nat's head. "Go take your meds," he said and headed for the door.

The woman who stood looking at him was a shadow of the woman they'd talk to the day before. Her arms wrapped around a box and a photo album, she smiled faintly.

She stepped inside and sniffed. "Do I smell coffee?"

"You certainly do." Harvey turned to the kitchen. "How do you take yours?"

"Two sugars and a splash of milk," she said. "Maybe three sugars this morning."

Behind him, Nat greeted Lenya. He glanced over at the women. Nat's hand rested on the sofa beside her. "Come, have a seat. We'll let you get some coffee into you before we talk."

"Sounds good." Lenya set her items on the coffee table and joined Nat.

Harvey doctored the hot java and after taking it to Lenya, settled in the armchair opposite the women. *Let them set the pace for the conversation.*

Lenya, leaning forward, jutted her chin toward the photo album. "What I found in those pictures..." She pressed her lips together. "It's more than I wanted to find."

Nat glanced at him and put an arm around Lenya. *Feeling her witnesses' moods and pain is both a blessing and a curse for her.* He did his best to offer both women silent support.

Lenya's sharp breath punctuated the moment. "Lily arrived, and we talked and dug out the old box Mom had kept. We found the picture album underneath it."

Harvey pointed at the picture album. "May I?"

Lenya nodded, her tension revealed by the myriad, tiny lines around her mouth and eyes.

Harvey reached for the book, and sitting back, opened it. He turned the pages carefully, examining each one thoroughly. A ruler marked one page. He glanced up at Lenya. "This one's important?"

She nodded. "Look closely at the center photo. You can see the necklaces."

Two girls in swimsuits were laughing into the camera, each wearing a silver chain and pendant. *Gloria and Amara.* He looked up. "Gloria's on the left?" *And they are in the old house.*

Lenya nodded.

Harvey showed the album to Nat. "Where was this taken? Do you know?"

Lenya's voice, husky with emotion, confirmed his guess. "Probably the old house. They used to hang out there a lot."

She slouched, her arms across her middle and her hands wrapping the opposite wrists. Age lines not there the day before framed her eyes. Tremors threatened around her mouth.

She's in her own kind of hell. They needed to give her time. "Lenya, did you eat this morning?" he asked.

"Eat? No, I don't think I did."

"Toast," he said. "Peanut butter or jam, or both?"

"Whatever is easier?"

"Both it is," he said.

Looking across the counter from the kitchen, he saw Nat take Lenya's hands. The two women sat quietly while he prepared the toast. Too much all at once had rendered more than one witness mute. *We need to take this easy.*

The silence settled and continued as Lenya accepted the toast and ate her way mechanically through it.

I bet she didn't taste a bite. Harvey took the empty plate, set it aside and reached for the box on the coffee table. "May I?" he asked again.

Lenya nodded and sank back against the cushions.

"Did...this belong to...Amara?" he asked.

"Yes. I didn't even know Mom had kept it."

Harvey opened the box. An advertising leaflet for a high school play, signed by the cast, lay on top. He lifted it out. "What part did Amara play?"

He barely heard her whispered reply. "She did stage setting."

"She was creative? Stage settings can be complicated."

"Oh yes." Lenya smiled. "No one could do the settings and backdrops like she did."

Harvey nodded, noting Lenya's returned smile. *Good memories help her.* He pulled out ticket stubs dated August 3, 1969. "Do you know what movie they saw?"

Lenya straightened. "Butch Cassidy and the Sundance Kid. They took me with them."

Nat glanced up. "I've never seen it. Did you like it?"

The touch of normal conversation seemed to dispel Lenya's stiffness further.

"An exciting story," Lenya said. "You'd like it, I think. Charismatic bad guys though."

Nat laughed. "But did the good guys win?"

"No spoilers from me," Lenya added. "You'll have to find a copy and watch it." She set down the mug. "Thanks for reminding me there were fun times. It makes it easier." She stretched out her hand and chose a black and white photo from the box.

Harvey sat back. *She's ready to tell the story herself.* He waited while she held it up.

"The Beatles," she said. "How Gloria loved their music." Another smaller photo came next. "Photo booth," Lenya announced. She passed the two joined pictures to Nat.

She examined them, touched one with a fingertip and passed them to Harvey.

He took them and gazed at the photo of two girls, their arms around each other, grinning out of the photo. *Gloria and Amara.* The necklaces were obvious against their shirts.

Time for a few questions. "Did they always wear the necklaces outside their shirts?"

"Only for these pictures. I think. I don't think Mom or Dad even knew about them."

But who did know? Had someone who never saw the pendants, but had seen the chains, made an assumption when identifying the body buried as Gloria?

The last item, a blue, square box had a label from *Peoples Jewellers, Ottawa.* The lid slid off easily, but the box was empty. He looked at Lenya.

She answered before he could ask. "Gloria brought it back with her when she came. The necklaces came in it." Lenya's voice cracked, and she cleared her throat.

"When did she get here?"

"In time for Amara's birthday. July seventh."

No wonder Mrs. Gerber hadn't recognized the necklaces. They were new and worn out of sight. *Lenya might be the only person who had known about them.*

****

Natalie watched Harvey set his recorder on the table. They needed the whole story. But what they had heard so far left Lenya looking wrung out. *We need a break here.*

"We do need to ask more questions." She nodded toward Harvey. "But maybe a timeout. And some hot chocolate with marshmallows to top off breakfast?"

"You bet," he agreed. "I'll put the kettle on."

The time break and sugared chocolate helped revive Lenya. She drained her drink and squared her shoulders. "Okay. Ask your questions. Let's get this over with."

Harvey switched on the recorder. "Narrative of events relayed by Lenya Conrad, nee Krause, of Caleb's Cove." He added the date and his and Natalie's rank and names. "Why don't you start when Gloria lived here and tell us everything you remember. Take your time. And if you need to stop, please tell us."

Lenya drew in a breath and expelled it noisily. "Gloria and Amara met in kindergarten. It didn't take long for them to become best friends. They stuck together through the grades. But when they were fourteen or so, Mr. Roberts started trying to keep them apart. For some reason, he no longer approved of their friendship. By then the Roberts family were living in a suite at the big house. They'd moved because Mr. Bockner didn't want to put any more money into the little house.

"Amara wasn't allowed to visit Gloria at the house. I don't know why not. Mr. Bockner wasn't there all winter. They'd come to our house after school, but Mr. Roberts would come for Gloria and ordered her to get in the car. I was afraid of him." She shuddered and stopped talking.

Ask her something ordinary. "How did you get home?"

Lenya smiled and answered easily. "The school bus brought us to the dock on the mainland and we'd come across by boat. When we were little, a parent came for us. Later, Lem ran the boat."

She fell silent again. "After Mr. Roberts started picking up Gloria, she and Amara countered by getting off the boat and running like crazy to hide. One time, Amara came home crying. She told me he'd hit Gloria when she got home. I didn't understand how a father could hit his daughter. But I know Amara worried about Gloria. When the school year finished, Mr. Roberts packed up the family and moved."

"How did Amara take it?" Nat asked, remembering Mrs. G.'s assessment.

"I'd never seen her so upset. She cried and screamed and wanted to go after them. She locked herself in the bedroom. I ended up sleeping on the couch in the living room. She didn't come out for days. Dad wanted to break down the door or go in through the window, but Mom said no. She tried everything she could think of to talk Amara into coming out. And one day a letter came from Gloria, and Amara came out. I figured things were back to normal."

Lenya gave a slight shake and focused on Harvey. "But it was only the beginning."

"What transpired afterward?" Harvey asked. "How did Amara make out when she returned to school?"

"She didn't mix much and she didn't find another close friend. She'd come home and spend hours writing letters and drawing pictures for Gloria. She finished Grade 12 and Mom wanted her to go to university. Amara said she'd only go if she could go to Carleton, in Ottawa, even if it took a lot of money."

How could kids make money on such a small island? "Did Amara have a summer job?" Natalie asked.

"She worked at the store for Mrs. Gerber. And helped Mom with the campground. She saved every penny and applied to Carleton, certain she'd get there."

"How did both girls end up here in 1969?" Harvey asked.

"July 7th, Amara's birthday, there came Gloria walking down the road. I was at the store when she walked in. Amara went crazy. They squealed and laughed and hugged each other. Looked like the original happy dance. They were happy." Lenya smiled at the memory.

This story is taking more twists than a tangled fishing line.

"Ottawa is almost fifteen hundred kilometers from here," Natalie said. "How did she get here? And did her parents, especially her father, know about her visit?"

"I'm not sure. She said they did. The first few nights Amara sent me back to the sofa and pulled my bed against hers for Gloria. Mom put an end to it. She set up a cot for me in the room and all three of us slept there. I heard Amara and Gloria whispering about her taking the bus to Halifax and hitching a ride down here. I don't think her father knew. Her mother, maybe."

Lenya's knuckles showed white. "Looking back, I remember things I wondered about but didn't get,"

"What things?"

"Well, when I got up in the morning and they were sleeping, they were holding hands and lying close, where the beds met. And when they got up they gave each other a good morning kiss."

Natalie frowned. "Kisses?"

"Like the French kisses - no, no, not the mouth kiss." Lenya hurried to clarify her meaning. "The kiss on each cheek. And they'd say, 'Friends forever,' like a vow."

Lenya stopped and Natalie allowed her space to think. Meanwhile, she turned the pages in the photo album, seeing the girls' photos, wondering what they'd felt and done. Her thoughts turned to their relationship. Quite extreme even for emotional teenagers. Had their attraction become physical?

Lenya gulped and started again. "Gloria worked for Mom at the campground while Amara worked at the store. They'd spend every suppertime and evening together, going on long walks until after dark. Those late walks upset Mom. But they were polite and they worked hard. And I know they kept their money in a can."

"But something went wrong," Natalie guessed.

"Mr. Roberts showed up." Lenya shivered. "He pulled up to the marina dock in a motor boat. I was behind what's now the café. His feet pounded on the boardwalk and crunched in the gravel. He stormed into the gas station." She shuddered again. "My heart jumped into my throat and stayed there. I didn't know if I should run and tell Amara or if my running to the store might show him where to go. I froze."

She stood and paced away from them, her arms stiff at her

sides. She kept her back to the room. "I edged around to the side and peeked." Her body bent forward and her head tipped. "He bolted from the gas station store. He got halfway to the grocery store and broke into a run. I looked across from me and saw Amara. She'd left the store by the back door. I knew she planned to go home.

"Roberts charged into the store and back out again pretty quick. He ran for the dock, his face so red I thought he'd have a heart attack. He jumped into the boat rocking it," she said, her body rocking with her words, "like crazy. He pulled the motor cord, threw off the line and roared away."

Lenya turned, close to hyperventilating.

Natalie went to her. "Breathe," she said, taking Lenya's hand, "we don't want you to have a heart attack."

Lenya wilted but took several deep breaths. Natalie led her back to the sofa. Lenya sank into the cushions and closed her eyes.

"I ran into the station and Mr. Harris let me call Mom. I was bawling and scared." Tears escaped from under her eyelids. "I told Mom what I'd seen. Then, I got on my bike and pedaled for home as fast as I could. When I got there, Mom stood on the canteen steps."

"And Mr. Roberts?"

"He stood looking up at her, shaking a fist and yelling bloody murder."

"And Gloria and Amara?"

"Gone. Not there. Mom stood with her feet apart, her arms crossed and her mouth all bunched up. If he'd known Mom better, he'd have realized he'd made a mistake when he threatened Amara."

Lenya managed a thin smile. "You didn't mess with Mom when it came to her children."

She sighed. "Anyway, Mom glared until he turned and stomped toward the campground dock. Before going through the trees, he turned back and yelled."

A sob escaped her. "*When I find those two little hussies, and I will, you'll never see them again.*"

The ugly, hostile words hung in the room.

Seconds ticked by.

Harvey leaned forward and turned off the recorder. "Lenya.

Telling your story wasn't easy for you. Thank you for sharing. And I'm sorry it's given you grief."

Lenya drew her brows together and pinched her lips. Her voice faded, losing power, and she delivered the end of the story. "I never saw Amara again." Tears ran down her face.

Nat hugged Lenya and pulled her close, cradling the older woman's head on her shoulder. She rubbed Lenya's back. Words roared in Natalie's head, but she couldn't find the right ones to say. She remembered her shock when her father died. Kind words had not penetrated her grief. Nothing anyone had said made any difference. *This is one of those times.*

CHAPTER EIGHT

Harvey left and returned with tissues.

Lenya managed a smile. "Seems you're always getting me tissues," she said.

Natalie pulled out a few and pressed them into her hands. "Come on." She tugged gently. "You'd do well with a sleep. You can go in my bed." The older woman didn't object and in minutes Natalie had removed Lenya's shoes and tucked the quilt around her. Lenya's breathing slowed and evened. And she slept.

Outside the room, Natalie stood with her forehead pressed against the door. *What a mess. What a heartache.* She turned away from the door.

Harvey met her in the living room and hugged her. She melted into his arms, welcoming the warmth and reassurance. "She has a tough memory to live with," he said. He rocked slightly. "I called Mrs. Roberts again. She has to be as old as Mrs. Gerber. I needed to make sure she's okay. Her story has to be equally harsh."

"And Mr. Roberts?" Natalie eased back and wrapped her arms around Harvey's waist.

"He died about two years ago, right before she moved back to Halifax."

"So does she have anyone to stay with her? To help her with the shock?"

"She has a nephew with her." He paused. "She said something interesting."

"About what?"

"The body in the grave. She said and I quote, 'I never quite believed the body was Gloria. It was her father agreed to the identification.'"

What an odd thing to say. Natalie hugged Harvey and stepped back. "Interesting and significant after what we just heard. Is she still willing to come and see us? If not, we could go to Halifax."

"She wants to come. She's having the nephew drive her down after she gives the DNA sample. She'll join us at the office."

Natalie ran her hand over the stubble on Harvey's face. Already it felt like a long day. Not only was she depleted emotionally, her body craved water. She drew a tall glass and drank it all in one go. "Okay, let's bring Devon up to speed and see what else happened on those two days."

"Vie will be over momentarily to stay with Lenya," he said. "And if FIS can't get down here anytime soon, I have an idea. We could get Adam's metal detector and do some preliminary searching. He's been bugging me to take him to the site."

"Definitely possible." Natalie stopped outside the front door. "And last, we need to talk to anyone who was here around August 16, 1969."

"What about updating Brayburn?" Harvey asked. "Do you think he'll allow more time?"

Natalie hemmed and hawed. "Later, much later, when we have more details, I'll call him. As for more time, I don't know. It may depend on what else is going on in Nova Scotia's world of crime."

Vie arrived. "What do you want me to do if she wakes?"

"Call me," Natalie said, "I'll come over. And maybe make her some tea." She managed to close the door behind her before she chuckled about the tea.

******* *

Harvey held Nat's hand all the way around the big house to the Caleb Cove Security Office and she didn't object. *Listening to Lenya's story has shaken her, too.* They went straight to the war room and stood, shoulder to shoulder and arms crossed, viewing the information pinned on the board.

Nat spoke first. "We need to do some rearranging. Collect what happened in the days leading up to their disappearance and fill in the gaps."

Footsteps sounded behind them. "I figured you might want a time line," Devon said, entering the room. "I went over all the news reports again." She rifled the cards like a dealer. "I have here, lady and gentleman, a rough time line."

Devon flipped the board over, revealing a cork board. She pinned up the August 1969 calendar. "From what you told me and based on other gathered information the girls were last seen on the evening of Friday, August 15th. Since the families figured they ran away, there wasn't much on the news about their leaving."

"However, here are the events happening in the province at that time. The Chester Race Week ran from August sixteenth to eighteenth." She pointed to 'Chester Race' already written on the calendar. "And the Canada Summer Games for 1969 were held in Dartmouth starting on August sixteen and running to the twenty-fourth."

She stopped and turned. "Did you know there used to be an island in Lake Banook? They drained the lake and bulldozed the island to make the lake usable for boat racing?"

Nat raised her eyebrows. "Interesting, but is it relevant?"

"Sorry. No." Devon turned back to her task. "From what the girls had said, everyone decided they were headed either for the Games or Woodstock. But, since they were late leaving, most folks figured they'd stop in Dartmouth. However, the police search turned up nothing." She added zeros to the appropriate dates before continuing.

"Mid-month, the southern US experienced a hurricane but it blew itself out before hitting Nova Scotia. There were high waves, but that was it. However," she said, pinning up a September map, "Hurricane Gerda went through September sixth to tenth, mostly in New Brunswick. But it produced high winds and power outages in Nova Scotia. Most likely there were some high seas as well. And that, folks, is when the body washed up on shore. The one they identified as Gloria Roberts." Devon put a red X on Monday, September eighth.

Nat applauded. "Way to go, Devon. That really narrows our time line."

Harvey grinned. *Nat has her mojo back.*

"We have arranged a talk with Mrs. Roberts. We both know the drill from here. Harvey, let's go talk to Lem. We need the Who, What, When, Where and Why of the fifteenth and sixteenth. And as the local historian, he's a good man to start with."

Nat tapped fingers against her chin. "And we need to find out who might have hung around with Gloria and Amara—locals, summer kids or hippies." She picked up her folder.

The phone rang and Devon answered. She listened and held the phone out to Nat. "It's Vie. Lenya is awake and having tea."

Nat took the phone. "Pour a cuppa for me," she said. "I'll be right over."

She waved the folder at Harvey. "Looks like you're on your own with Lem. I'll see what Lenya can tell us about the search for the girls. Call me when you hear from Mrs. Roberts." She turned to Devon and explained. "So if Mrs. Roberts arrives first, bring her here and," Nat said, doing a one-two dance step, "give her some tea."

"Good luck." Devon raised a hand. "And do learn things, kiddies."

****

Twenty minutes later, Lenya, clear eyes and decreased under-eye shadows revealing her renewed mood, sat in the cabin's living room.

Natalie set down her cup and leaned forward. "I've read the news accounts," she said, sparing Lenya from having to relay those details. "However, now that we're dealing with a murder or an illegal disposal of a body, we have to ask questions they wouldn't have asked in 1969."

Lenya straightened her shoulders. "I've been thinking. I'm sure a murdered body needs different background checks than an accidental death." She sighed deeply. "Ask away. We all need closure, one way or another."

"Thanks," Natalie said. "We need all the information anyone can remember." She filled Lenya in on Mrs. Roberts, DNA, and research. She indicated the recording mode on her phone. "I'm recording the conversation," she said and added date, time and persons present.

"Lenya, you last saw Amara running from the grocery toward home. Do you know if anyone else saw Gloria Roberts or Amara Krause after they left your mother?"

"I don't think so. Mom and Dad didn't tell me much, probably to spare me. But I'd rather have known. What I do know is, they scoured the island. They checked with Mr. Harris at the marina to see if the girls had taken a boat off the island. And they went to the bus depots in Bridgewater and Lunenburg. When they didn't find them, they went to the police and reported Amara missing and believed to be with Gloria."

"Did the police search as well? And Mr. Roberts?" Natalie asked.

"The police posted bulletins and put an alert on the radio. Mr. Roberts did the same as Mom and Dad."

"And no one reported seeing them?"

"I don't think so. The next thing I knew, the police got a call about a body washed up on the mainland." Lenya looked at her hands clasped in her lap. "I'll never forget my parents' grief and my mother's tears. The way she jumped every time the phone rang. But the call never came. We never found Amara."

"Thank you. Ending this interview at ten forty-seven a.m."

Natalie stood and stepped close to Lenya, laying a hand on her shoulder. "I'm sorry to drag this all up for you." She looked into her eyes. "We'll sort it out. And do the best we can to find out the truth. Once we have a DNA match to Gloria Roberts, we'll look for Amara up on the hill."

Lenya wrapped her fingers together. "So you think Amara might be buried up there, too?"

"Officially, I can't say. But, she might be." Natalie stood. "There is a slim chance the body isn't Gloria. I'll let you know as soon as I can."

"It's horrible if they were buried up there all these years. But, whoever is there, she can have a proper burial. She can, can't she? I mean if we find Amara, we can rebury her properly, right? Mom would have liked it."

"I don't see why not. Give us time."

Lenya stood and hugged Natalie. "Thanks. It's great to have you involved in this. I wouldn't want anyone else handling it. I know you care, we all know."

"I do," Natalie said. She walked Lenya to her car and saw her on her way. *But I hope Brayburn agrees I should stay on the case.*

****

Natalie lingered in the parking area, closing her eyes against the sun but welcoming the warmth. With Mrs. Roberts arriving, and Harvey interviewing Lem, hope for useful information ran high. Identifying the girl at least put them on the correct path. The heat flowed through her, relaxing her muscles and renewing her energy. *Is Harvey back yet?* She opened her eyes. *No car. Maybe Lem has a lot to say.*

Her phone rang ending the calm moment.

"Parker," she said.

Brayburn's voice blasted in her ear. "What the bloody hell is going on down there?"

Natalie's arm jerked, removing the phone from close proximity to her ear. "Pardon?"

Spitting mad, Brayburn continued. "That blasted video went viral and makes us all look like fools. Especially you."

"What video?"

Brayburn coughed, not bothering to cover the mouthpiece. "Get yourself to a computer. Check the news channels. They've picked it up. Call me once you've seen it. I have questions. And make it snappy."

What the heck? Natalie sprinted across the asphalt and took the three steps to the offices in one jump. She burst through the door.

Devon, standing in the main room watching the TV screen, turned to meet her. She pointed the channel changer and muted the sound. "Ah, I see you've heard about the You Tube video." She raised the changer and turned up the sound.

"And, folks." The announcer's mellow voice flowed into the room. "What is our police force up to in Caleb's Cove? It's a tiny community with a record number of crimes and a touch of police hanky-panky." He paused. "Or so the video that's gone viral on YouTube says." He slid a page to the side and started on the next news item.

Devon muted the sound.

Natalie sank onto the edge of the sofa and glared straight ahead.

Devon voiced what Natalie was thinking "A spy was watching

us, taping our moves and recording our conversations."

Natalie gripped her forehead with one hand. "How could it happen? We don't discuss the case in public."

"Well, my guess is that the snoop, whoever he or she is, has been lurking in the woods and under windows, or," Devon said, tossing the changer onto the sofa, "using a device to pick up our conversations."

This is unbelievable. "That is illegal."

"True. But legal or not, it's happened."

Oh crap, no wonder Brayburn's blood pressure was through the roof. "Who posted the video?"

"The news didn't say. And apparently, police officials are making no comment until they investigate. Wait," Devon said, "I'll play the YouTube version for you."

She flipped through the screens until the video came up. Natalie braced herself. The view panned the woods and rocks until it focused on the overturned tree and its roots. The lens moved closer. Light picked up the direct dig. A hand appeared and brushed away dirt until a bone appeared.

Dismay shot through her. "That has to be the person who was there the first night. The one who stepped into the existing footprints. How did he know to go there? The report wasn't released until the next morning."

In a whispered voice often heard on ghost videos and séances, a man's voice kept up a commentary." Natalie winced. The narrator outlined Mutt's find, the search, and the final discovery. He noted that Chief Superintendent Curwood had seen fit to check on Constable Parker. Conrad and the FIS team were also mentioned.

Oh blue baby ducks. This is indefensible.

Another shot showed an angle of the café's interior and focused on Rob eating his breakfast. The voice identified him as the forensics technician on the case.

Not too bad. So far nothing the public couldn't have seen for themselves. *Maybe it'll even flush out a witness or two from 1969.*

The accompanying narrative stated Rob's name, rank, and qualifications and the fact he'd spent the night in the FIS trailer. It detailed his breakfast at the café, he had bacon and eggs. But as far the reporter could tell, Rob had left the trailer unattended.

"That's a lie," Natalie burst out. "Turner watched the van."

The narrator glanced at his notes before looking into the camera. "As near as the evidence can tell--"a pregnant pause left room for doubt--"they found a body, one that's been unlooked for and missed for years. Currently, it's being moved to Halifax, and we await further information on the body's identity.

Natalie muttered under her breath. "Oh crap. No, no, no, please don't let them have a name or the information about the mistaken identity of the woman in the grave."

In the next video sequence, Harvey helped Natalie up the walk to Cabin Three. Natalie sprang off the sofa-arm, a less than ladylike expression echoing in her head. The video panned the front of the cabin as the exterior lights came on. She pressed one fist against her mouth and the other against her midriff.

"Constable Natalie Parker," the creepy voice announced, "is recently back on the job after an explosion, and a resulting concussion, which put her in hospital." A deep breath, almost a sigh echoed in the mike. "Has she returned to work too soon?"

Now that is bad. Her mother's voice haunted her. *'Oh, what a web you weave, when at first you practice to deceive.'* She'd always got the quote wrong. *I'm dead meat.*

Sunlight lit the next sequence, and the voice announced morning. Cabin Three and Lenya carrying the photo album and box flashed on the screen. "This reporter poses the question, 'what evidence does the campground owner bring with her?'"

On screen, Harvey answered the door to let Lenya in.

"Not to speak ill of our law enforcement, but to the best of this reporter's knowledge, both officers remained in the cabin all night. We will provide updates as the story unfolds." And the nosy, lying excuse for a reporter signed off.

Natalie's phone rang. Expecting Brayburn, she tensed. "Yes."

Harvey's voice, back-dropped by a running engine, asked, "Have you...?"

Natalie cut in. "Yes, the bloody, sniveling, little snot. Can they track him with the IP address?"

"It's the public IP address at the campground. However, the news station did help. I'm on my way to the campground now. The snoopy photographer is staying there. I'll have a chat with him, maybe run him in. Depends on how he got his information."

"Thanks. You're calmer about this than I am." Natalie hung up and turned to Devon. "What a mess."

Oh crap. Brayburn. How the heck can I placate him after this?

CHAPTER NINE

The newscast moved to other stories and flickered across the screen above them. "What now?" Devon asked.

"Now I face Brayburn. He's called already and he's not happy." Natalie paced the room, her arms wrapped around her middle. Her stomach soured and her heart drove her pulse faster. The roar in her ears threatened a headache. *Not the time.*

"He could suspend you, couldn't he?" Devon stepped up and put a hand on Natalie's forearm.

Natalie dragged both hands over her face. *What a mess.* "Oh yes. And Harvey is in for it, too. I'd put a year's salary on us being taken off the case for sure." *What else can we expect?*

"Will they assign someone else?"

A flicker started in the corner of her eyelid. She pressed two fingers against it. "I don't know. They could simply ID the body, release it for re-burial and put solving the case on the cold case list until someone has time."

"Not acceptable." Devon's tone brooked no nonsense. She squared her shoulders. "Let's focus here. What is *likely* to happen?"

Natalie closed the eye with the annoying tic. "Suspension for me." She pointed at the war room. "All this evidence boxed and transferred to Halifax." A wry grin twisted her lips. "Harvey might get off with traffic duty. But either way, I can see this going south fast."

"Not if I can help it." Devon turned and stomped toward the evidence display. "You go on back to the cabin and call your boss. I'll handle this."

"What...?"

Devon waved her hand over her head without turning. "Ask no

questions, I'll tell you no lies. Now go."

Natalie went. She blocked her thoughts from heading after Devon. She didn't want to know Devon's plan. *At least not now.* She marched across the parking lot and around to the cabin. She needed to think like a constable.

Paused at her temporary lodgings, she drew in a deep breath. Frustration with the male world and officious bosses rolled through her. And not for the first time. She expelled the breath slowly. *Time to face the music.*

Inside she adjusted her belt, planted her feet slightly apart and pulled out her phone. *I need to stand to face this one. And I need to be brutally honest - no matter how it makes me look.*

Brayburn answered on the first ring. "Took you long enough."

"A lot to consider, sir."

"And none of good."

Well, not everything looked bad.

"What do you have to say?"

Take a long walk off a short dock.

She focused. "First, let's address the outright lie in the video. Rob did not leave the trailer and site unattended. Constable Turner from the local detachment replaced him."

Brayburn's habitual grunt echoed in the phone.

"And we never discussed this in any public location. If this reporter has information from private discussions, and it seems he or she does, they used illegal means to get it. Conrad is dealing with it now."

"However, they got it, it's out there causing damage," Brayburn said. "We'll deal with the reporter, but doing so won't erase the image already created in the public forum."

"Yes, sir, you're right. No, sir, it won't erase it."

"Now, Parker, what's this about you and Constable Conrad?"

She tightened her abdominals to help control her voice. "Nothing untoward, sir. We are both using the cabin, which has two very private bedroom suites and a shared living room and kitchen. You gave me two days, sir. We've simply been trying to maximize the time."

Brayburn stayed silent for long moments. "And why did you require assistance to get into the cabin?"

"Just a headache, sir."

"And was this before or after I asked if you were okay?"

Parker drew in a breath as silently as possible. "After, sir, but you never asked about headaches."

"I'll give you one thing, Parker. You're good at seemingly logical explanations and hair-splitting. However, I'm not totally convinced about any of it. The main office called." He took a breath.

The main office means Chief Superintendent Curwood. I am well and truly hooped.

"And it's been decided we'll suspend this case until things die down. We will let the parts already in play continue to a logical conclusion. Then we'll assign it to the cold case list."

Exactly what I expected.

"As you wish, sir. I'll wrap…"

"You'll. Do. Nothing. Except take a one-month suspension. See the doctor and the shrink who cleared you too early for field duty. I warned you what would happen if you screwed up. We'll revisit whether your actions have been lackadaisical, or outright incompetent, later."

She swallowed hard. "Sir."

"Curwood and the computer tech team from Bridgewater will be there later this morning to pack up whatever you have and bring it here. Papers, photos, notes, computer data—everything."

Natalie gulped. *Damn it*. Even though she'd expected it, she'd hoped it wouldn't happen.

"And give your gun and shield to Curwood with the data. Got it?"

"Yes, sir." She snapped her free hand to her forehead in a mock salute. *Whatever you say, sir.*

And the phone slammed in her ear. Constable Natalie Parker stared at the phone in her hand. The end, over, done, finished.

****

Natalie punched the fast dial for Harvey's phone.

Like Brayburn, he answered on the first ring. "Nat? What's up?"

"At the moment, I am officially off the job. One month

suspension. Ordinary citizen. Pending investigation."

Harvey's under-breath curse barely reached her. "Sweetheart, you are far from ordinary anything. What about the case?"

Natalie paced to the kitchen and opened the fridge. "Good policeman that he is, Brayburn says he'll let it run until the identity is confirmed, and file it as a cold case."

Wordless time hung between them, punctuated by the humming fridge on her end, and the road noise on Harvey's end.

Maybe an apple. Natalie retrieved one and shut the door. "On the other matter," she said, "did you find the disruptive video maker?"

A faint click signaled his turn indication. "Oh, yes. Turner and I are on the way to the detachment with him, his camera and his parabolic equipment."

"So he did cheat." She moved the phone away from her mouth and bit into the apple.

"Sure did. Turner will process him." A slight pause. "I have a meeting with my boss."

"Oh, boy. How much trouble do you think you're in?" *Damn, I didn't think ahead on this one. Not only are my actions in question. So are Harvey's.*

"I know what you're thinking. Don't go there. Anything I did, I did with full knowledge and free choice. This whole cock-up was caused by the twists the video maker put on things." The road noise stopped. "I have a plan. I'm due a vacation, I think now is an opportune time to ask for it. Save the boss the trouble of deciding what to do with me."

Nat sat at the counter and took another bite of the apple. Juice spurted in her mouth, sweet and soothing. "Vacation time does look better on your records than a suspension." She sighed. "Although it messes with our vacation plans." She swallowed.

"You're eating," Harvey said. "You must be distressed. Take it easy." He chuckled. "We'll figure out something for vacation. I won't use it all." The road noise resumed, and a car horn sounded. They were on the move again.

Natalie strolled to the patio doors and contemplated the green grass and bright sunlight all backed by dancing trees. *All is well in the world. And we will weather this blow-up. One way or the other.*

"Good luck," she said. "I'm heading back to the CCSA office

to see what Devon is up to."

"She's up to something?"

"'Ask me no questions and I'll tell you no lies.' Then she booted me out. What do YOU think?"

He laughed out loud. "I think I don't want to know before I talk to my boss."

"My thoughts exactly," Natalie said. "Okay - talk soon. Let me know how it goes."

"Keep your chin up," Harvey said. "There's always a solution, and I'll bring pizza for supper."

Natalie placed the phone on the counter and leaned forward on her elbows. She hooked her feet in the stool rungs and sighed. Such simple things knitted together to portray misconduct. She knew Brayburn couldn't be seen to condone what was suggested. And now Curwood was involved, they'd decided it was an untenable situation.

Her lips stretched flat and her gut tightened. *Resentment, that's what I'm feeling. Looks like I don't like taking orders anymore.*

She'd devoured the apple before her brain offered a solution. *So, don't. Find a way to be your own boss. Or at least find a team where you will be treated equally.*

Natalie Ann Parker tossed the apple core in the compost bin and, picking up her phone, headed for the door. *Now there's an idea worth considering.*

****

In no hurry to face a de-frocking as it were, Natalie strolled back to the office. She didn't want to have to tell Lenya, when the time came, about the police putting the case on hold. The burgeoning idea of leaving law enforcement prodded her. *A lot going on between my ears.*

To be honest, after the explosion and her stay in hospital, she'd considered other options. But back then, it was because she didn't know if she could handle going back. Or maybe her inner child had already yearned for other adventures. *I'll talk to Harvey about it tonight.*

Thinking about Harvey left her grinning as she reached the

office steps. *If I'm no longer in law enforcement, we wouldn't have to be so cautious.*

Devon looked at her and held up a hand, palm out. "Hang on - go sit on the veranda for about fifteen more minutes." She pushed a box under the coffee table with her foot.

"What on earth for?"

"You are suspended, you can't go in the war room. I'm busy so don't disturb me. And it's a nice day out. Enough reasons, don't you think?"

Natalie looked at the ceiling, counted to ten. "Fine already. But I'm not going outside, I'm going looking for tea and cookies."

"Wow. You? Voluntarily looking for tea? This whole thing does have you rattled."

Natalie flipped Devon off. "Don't tell grandma how to suck eggs." Once in the hall, she smelled baking. Vie must have heard the news. She baked for every event, big or small, good or bad.

The kitchen door gave under her touch and she peered around it. "Need a cookie tester?" she asked.

Vie glanced up from stacking cookies into a tin. Three more tins sat on the work island, each with a different cookie variety inside. "Sure, I'm about done. I'll get you a mug of tea to wash them down."

Minutes later Natalie perched at the work island, facing the fancy tins and tea. "Do you think there's such a job as taster in a cookie factory?" she asked Vie.

"Could be. But it wouldn't be good for your health."

Natalie sighed. "Worse than getting blown up followed by screwing up?"

"Pshaw. You're fine. It's those uptight policemen bosses." Vie emphasized the police part. "And too many rules and regulations, a lack of ethics in news people and the gullibility of the population in general."

Nat coughed around the cookie and took a hurried sip of tea. "I've never heard you say so much all at once."

Vie sniffed. "I read the news online and listen to the radio. I have my opinions. And if we could blow up the bridge between here and the mainland and still survive, it'd be a darn good thing to do." She poured herself a tea and sat opposite Nat. "And your officious bosses, putting you on suspension. You're the best investigator they've got. You could start your own detective agency and get rich without them."

Natalie tipped her head. "I don't think private investigators get rich." *But the other part of it appealed. No one to boss her around. Her choice of cases. Not a bad idea.*

Vie waved a hand around the room. "This crew is doing quite well."

"True, but they do hi-profile security which brings in big bucks, and I do believe Greg and Devon bought this place outright."

"Still, you should think about it. I know the folks around here would hire you. And goodness knows, enough crazy things happen around here, they could use you."

"Vie, you're good for my confidence. Thank you."

"Pshaw," Vie said again. "And if you ever need one, me and Frank, we'll give you a reference."

Before the conversation could continue, Devon waltzed into the room. "Okay, you're ready to face the dragon. Stand back and let them take what they want."

Natalie put her head in both hands. "Oh goodness, what have you done?"

"Me?" Devon clasped her hands behind her back and rocked on her feet. "Nothing. Just housekeeping."

Natalie held up a hand, palm out. "Never mind. I don't want to know. Sounds boring."

"Could be."

A chimed tune played through the house. "The beasts are at the door," Devon said. "How polite of them to ring. Law enforcement doesn't always."

Natalie headed for the hall. "I'll greet them before they try breaking and entering." She looked back. "Are you coming?"

Devon shook her head. "Better if you do it. Besides there are cookies." She waved Nat on her way. "I'll pick up the pieces later."

CHAPTER TEN

Before she reached the office door, Natalie squared her shoulders, braced her back and stilled her face. *It's only business. I can do this.* She envisioned them in their underwear, the way she used to see audiences when she first did public speaking. It helped—a bit.

Curwood headed the procession. He nodded at her and stood back to let the others inside. "Office is there," he said, pointing. "War room is there. Check everything, take it all."

The three men headed to their respective areas and Curwood turned to Parker. "Constable, it's too bad things came to this, but here we are. You and I need a private chat, and I'd like to see your quarters."

Natalie indicated her agreement. "This way," she said and headed out. "We go around here to the cabins." She marched, looking neither to right or left.

Curwood took in the area. "These are the cabins Dr. Zinck put in for his recovering patients?"

"Yes, sir."

"Handy for guests," he stated, "or for visiting police officers."

That sounds snarky. She stopped and faced him. "Is there a problem, sir? These people are friends and colleagues. They nursed me back to health in this cabin. They make it available to me as a close friend and as a police officer."

He pulled back a fraction. "No problem." He started walking again. "So, you'll stay on here?"

"Not sure, sir. I do have appointments I'll need to make in the city." She headed for cabin three. "But it is great weather, and I am currently without any tasks. Perhaps I will stay and do some sailing."

"You're rather blasé for someone who has been suspended and with possible charges pending."

"Would you rather I wail and shed tears?"

"No need to get snippy, Constable."

She made no return remark. Given the circumstances, she might as well be as snippy as she liked. Standing in the cabin foyer, she outlined the layout. "One bedroom suite, living room and kitchen, second bedroom suite. There are patio doors to the yard. It leads up to the old house. Handy during our investigation. Full internet services for computers and research."

"And is there any case material here or on your computer?"

"No, sir. I transferred all reports to Brayburn as I wrote them and the copies are on the server over in the offices. Nothing stored here."

Curwood opened the doors to the bedrooms, looked out the patio door and returned to where she stood by the front door. "I need your badge and gun," he said, holding out his hand.

Not even a please or may I?

"Yes, sir." *Anything else, sir.* She unclipped her badge and pulled her gun from the holster under her jacket. *Won't miss the holster and jacket - I can be much cooler without them.* She removed the bullets. *One clip full, sir.*

Butt-end first, she handed him the gun with one hand and the bullets and badge with the other. He pulled an evidence bag from his pocket and stored her signs of authority.

"Thank you, Parker. We have everything we need."

So now he uses my name. But no title.

She followed him into the yard.

"I think you better stay here," Curwood said. "We'll be in touch." And he marched off, his cocky parade walk showing.

Why do I find him so annoying? Between him and Brayburn, I could scream.

****

Harvey exited the Bridgewater Detachment and stopped on the top step. Turner was booking the overzealous photographer-cum-reporter, a cocky eighteen-year-old in Caleb's Cove to film the

Junior Dory Races. He should have stuck to boats and oarsmen.

Apparently, all departments were shelving the Caleb's Cove case for the time being. If they got a positive ID on the body, they'd store all items deemed to be evidence and allow the mother to bury the bones. The higher powers decided the body's fifty or so years interred in dirt made it a cold case. As in they would not probably solve it anyway.

And me? Where do I stand? He clattered down the concrete steps and headed for his personal vehicle. *My three-week vacation leave is better than Nat's suspension. Unfortunately, I am not good at vacations.*

In the car, Harvey inserted the ignition key but sat back. Should he head straight for the Cove? Go home for clothing more suitable for vacationing? Or confer with Nat? The last action won the toss. He retrieved his phone and pushed the one digit needed to connect him to her.

Three rings and she answered. "Hey, what's the verdict?"

Harvey rested his head on the headrest and smiled. *Her voice is as good as a tonic.* "Better than you. I got the vacation leave. Any other action will depend on what my boss finds out. He's going over the case with guys from your office."

"Are they going to pursue it?" Natalie asked.

He wished he could tell her yes. "No, they're double-checking us. And making sure the evidence isn't contaminated in any way."

"Bummer," Nat said. "This girl's family, whoever they are, deserves to know what happened."

Always the bottom line for Nat. Give the family closure. He heard a door shut. "You're still headed down here?" she asked. "And bringing some shorts? I'd like to check out your legs."

"Gee, thanks. I'm going to run some errands, but as promised, I'll bring pizza for supper. We can go over last week's details." He cleared his throat which didn't need clearing. "In case we need to defend our reputations."

"Excellent. And tomorrow let's take a sail, let the breezes blow away the cobwebs and let the dust settle before making any decisions." Her voice sounded wistful.

Harvey put some smile in his voice. "I hear you. A day off isn't always a bad thing. But only one day, eh?"

Her agreement came easily. "For sure. Perhaps there are things we can do, to keep us busy, right?"

She's thinking what I'm thinking. We know people who might be connected and we know them as friends, we can talk to them about anything we like.

"Now," Nat said, "I'm going to walk on the beach. I need to work off all off Vie's cookies and I've some thinking to do."

"Enjoy. I'll see you later." He disconnected, leaned forward and started the car. *She's perfect as she is, no matter how many cookies she eats.* He left the parking lot. *And definitely smart. Between us, we'll find a way to work around her suspension and my vacation. Even if we shouldn't.*

****

Later than he'd planned, Harvey reached Caleb's Cove. He stood on the step with the pizza in one hand and his overnight case in the other. *Can't open the door with no hands.* He used his toe to knock.

Nat opened the door so fast she must have been waiting beside it.

"Food. About time."

He held the pizza over his head. "Not so fast."

She gave him a kiss on the cheek and took the pizza. "I'm starving."

"It's a cook-at-home one," he said. "The readymade ones would have been cold by the time I got here."

She turned toward the kitchen. "Let's get this cooking underway."

"Go for it. I'll stow my gear." He grabbed the bag and headed for his room. By the time he returned, the oven was preheating.

He joined her in the kitchen and leaned against the work island, stuck in a toothpick and watched her find the proper pan. "Walking on the beach must be a good appetite raiser."

"Hmm," she said and slid the pizza onto the round pan. She turned to him and raised her glass. "Tea, coffee or…"

He waggled his eyebrows. "Isn't the ending of the saying—or me?"

She shook her forefinger at him. "Don't be fresh. The choices are either iced tea or wine."

Not quite as appealing. "What are you having?" he asked.

She sighed. "Tonight I want my head clear. I'm into the homemade iced tea Vie brought over."

"Homemade! Why didn't you say so? Iced tea it is."

Taking their glasses with them, they adjourned to the sofa. Not so close they touched, although he'd have liked her nestled in at his side. He turned sideways and extended his arm along the sofa back until his fingers rested lightly on her shoulder in his habitual move.

He tweaked her collar. "How was the walk? And the thinking?"

Nat ran her finger around the lip of her glass. "Good walk. The thinking, on the other hand, is complicated."

Shadows lurked in her eyes, and he returned his fingers to her shoulder. "How so?"

"It's about work. After the concussion, my nerves almost did me in. And after the desk duty, I almost didn't ask for clearance for field work. Remember?"

He remembered it all clearly. The explosion and concussion shook her badly. "Mm."

"But I did go back and I did get clearance for field work." She snorted. "And here I am, suspended. However, I know I can do the job. I need to watch for those headaches, but I can do it."

He watched her pick lint on her jeans. A habit signaling her thinking mode. "I sense you have a 'but'," he said. "What is it?"

"I might not want to stay on the police force. Maybe it's all that has happened recently, but I have a been-there, done-that feeling. And during my walk, I remembered what I planned to be when I grew up. It wasn't a police officer." She looked up at him imploringly. "What do you think?"

Harvey brushed the backs of his fingers over her cheek, and she trapped his hand against her shoulder. "Listen to your thoughts and your gut. But kids do change their minds. What did you think you'd be?"

She raised the forefinger again. "Don't laugh. Promise."

He crossed his chest. "Promise." And he knew he'd better keep the promise. What had the thirteen-year-old Natalie wanted to be that might trigger laughter?

"A ventriloquist."

He coughed in a hurry. His thoughts had run to nurse or teacher or even an explorer, but not a ventriloquist.

She swatted his shoulder. "You promised not to laugh."

He waved a hand in defense. "Not laughing. I am surprised though. It's an unusual career aspiration."

She grinned. "I know. Not many kids want to be ventriloquists. But I was good at it. I even won some middle school talent shows."

From ventriloquism to law enforcement. Losing her father obviously changed the course of her life. "What shifted for you when your dad died?"

"As a police officer, he made a difference for people. He talked about giving clarity to a victim's family. He never forgot a case, even if it dried up and got stuck in the cold case box. He'd pull things out as new forensics came to light. And he always said given time, everyone talks." She closed her eyes and sat still for long moments. "I think I wanted to take his place."

Nat reached around and set her empty glass on the end table. "And when he was murdered on the job they never solved it. Nobody stuck with it for him, or for us—me, and Mom, and Travis. They never even found his body." She pressed her fist against her chest bone. "I still feel it here. The not knowing makes it worse."

Harvey thought back to his reasons for joining the police. Hers were as valid if not more valid, than his. "So you became a police officer. Isn't your brother one?"

Nat nodded. "But he planned to be one long before Dad died. I met Sam and Greg because of Travis. Their friendship grew from their plans to go into law enforcement. For various reasons, both Sam and Greg eventually decided to go private."

"But your brother, Travis, stayed in?"

"Um huh, he's still on the Calgary force."

Two police officers in the family. I wonder how their mother feels about it after having a husband killed in the line of duty. "And looking back, what do you think?"

"I think I needed to do what I needed to do. But the police force is no longer for me." She crossed her arms. "This incident, with them putting the case on a back burner, is I suppose, the pebble that sinks the boat, as Lem says. Even if it is an old case, and manpower is stretched to the limit, someone should figure out what happened to the girl. And if it's Gloria, we should be considering what happened to Amara. I know my father would not have given up."

Harvey set down his glass and pulled both her hands into his. They were ice cold. He rubbed them to warm them up. "Whatever you do," he said. "I've got your back, remember."

She leaned in and kissed him. "And I am forever grateful."

He tucked both her hands firmly in his. "Have you thought about what you might do? Or are you still keen on the ventriloquist thing?"

She ducked her head. "I've put a request out to the universe for some ideas."

This time he did laugh and kissed her in return. "You'll know when the right thing comes along."

"Hey, don't laugh, it works. Maybe it's because the directive makes our brains notice things, but it works."

Harvey shifted in his seat and tugged gently until she turned and rested against his chest, her head back on his shoulder, her feet up on the sofa. "Fair enough. And as for the case we've been so unceremoniously tossed off, Turner should be calling soon. He headed for FIS today and planned to find out the DNA results. We can at least keep tabs on what's happening."

She wiggled, snuggling against him. "He'll do that?"

"Sure. I'm technically on vacation, remember, not blackballed. And, for your information, one task I took care of before I left town, was to call Mrs. Roberts. I wanted to be the one to tell her the case will be shelved."

"Did you reach her? Is she okay?" Nat asked.

"She'd seen the crazy video. We decided she wouldn't come down tomorrow."

"But…" Nat stopped. "Drat, I guess questioning her is out."

"Yes and no." Harvey rubbed a hand down her arm. "She still wants to come to the Cove." He drummed his fingers against her wrist. "And there's no reason we can't have tea with her and listen to her talk about the past."

The oven bell noisily interrupted. Natalie struggled off the sofa and headed for the kitchen. He let her go reluctantly.

She groaned as she closed the oven door. "Twenty-five minutes more. I'll starve!" She rejoined Harvey.

"Come here, I'll distract you." He was content to let her sit with her back against him and rest her head on his shoulder. The timer ticked away in the kitchen. The pizza odors wafted into the room. *Where are we going from here? Without a case, can we talk about us for a change?* He closed his eyes and tipped his head against Nat's. *It's time, past time.*

****

Devon burst into the room, not bothering to knock. "Have you two got a few minutes?"

Harvey, jolted from his semi-doze, rubbed his eyes. "All the time in the place," he said and yawned.

Devon laid a finger alongside her nose. "Not for long."

Natalie swung her feet to the floor and sat upright. "And what is that supposed to mean?"

"I have a plan."

Natalie planted a hand on her forehead. "Oh heavens, one of your plans." She shuddered.

Harvey's phone rang, and he answered, forestalling further questions. "Turner, what have you got?"

Devon perched on the chair across from the sofa, raised her shoulders and stretched out her hands, silently questioning.

Harvey deliberately kept his replies ambiguous. "Okay. Good enough. Sure, I'll tell her." He ended the call.

Nat poked him when he didn't speak immediately. "So, what did he say?"

Harvey gave her his best serious look. "He said to say he hoped you were okay. He's worried about you."

With another poke in his midriff, she leaned in further. "That's not what I meant and you know it."

Harvey grabbed the poked spot and relented. "The DNA is a match. Our forgotten girl is Gloria Roberts."

"We were right," Natalie said. "I'm not happy about who it is. But if knowing the victim points us in the direction of the killer, it's a good find. Too bad we can't follow through."

Devon coughed but Harvey ignored her.

"There is more," he said, "Rob finished the house inspection and the subsequent tests. He chatted with Turner. The blood in the kitchen also matches. Gloria Roberts died in the old house and was buried in the yard. All we need now is to figure out who did it."

Nat stood and paced. "And if Brayburn has his way, we might never know. Right now, there are still people alive who were around in 1969. Leave it too long, and there might be no one to talk to."

Devon jumped out of the chair and clapped her hands. "And here's where my plan comes in," she said. "We have to connect to Greg and Sam." She looked at her watch. "In half an hour, once I tell you the plan. We need to go over to the office, right now."

"Devon!" Nat stopped and stared at her. "What are you up to?"

Devon zipped her mouth with two fingers.

Is she up to another Caleb's Cove caper to circumvent law enforcement? Natalie looked at Harvey and crossed her eyes.

He joined her and dropped an arm over her shoulders. "We might as well go and listen," he said.

They were almost out the door when Natalie froze. "The pizza."

Devon stopped. "I suspected I smelled pizza, but I assumed you'd eaten. We can wait for it to finish."

"And I suppose you'll help eat it?"

"You'll share with a friend who's going to put you back in business, won't you?"

Harvey laughed. "You two do love your food."

The two women did an about face and headed to the kitchen. Harvey followed.

Nat checked the timer. "Only three minutes left."

Devon opened the lower cabinets and rooted around until she found a platter. "We'll take it with us and eat over there."

Harvey picked up the hot mitts. The timer buzzed. "Open the door, Nat. I'll get the pizza. Have to admit, Devon, I am curious about your plan."

CHAPTER ELEVEN

Outside the cabin, dusk had descended, bringing with it a heavy mist. Natalie curled her shoulders and glanced at the eastern sky. Dark clouds loomed and radiating grayness showed rain in the distance. *If it hits land, it'll turn the grave into a huge puddle.*

"We'll cut through the house," Devon said and hustled across the cabin veranda, the gravel perimeter and the large deck behind the house. In the kitchen, Devon skirted the work island, plucked paper towels off the counter and headed for the hall. Minutes later they were in the offices.

"The war room first," Devon said and led the way to the closed door. She put her hand on the knob but looked back. "Close your eyes," she said.

"Devon, what's with the cloak and dagger bit?" Natalie asked.

"Just do it."

Natalie glanced at Harvey. He'd already closed his. She obliged Devon and closed hers. A click indicated an opening door.

Devon took Natalie's elbow and pulled. "No peeking."

A whiff of pizza tickled Natalie's nose. *Harvey and the pizza have entered the room.*

The air eddied slightly. *Devon moving?*

"Ready," Devon said. "On a count of three open your eyes. One, two and three."

Natalie opened her eyes, her head turned to Devon.

Devon pointed at the other side of the room.

Natalie looked. The evidence board, looking like it had that morning, looked back at her. *But they took all that.* "I saw them packing it up."

Beside her, Harvey whistled. "How did you sweet talk them

out of this?"

"Didn't," Devon said. "It's amazing what I can do with a photocopier, a good phone camera and time."

Natalie stared at her. "You do know that is quite likely illegal."

Devon held a hand parallel to the floor and rocked it. "Yes and no."

Harvey coughed around a laugh. "Look at the header," he said to Natalie. He read aloud. "CCSA, Missing person's case re Amara Krause."

"It's a new case," Devon said. "But that's no reason to let good information go to waste."

Natalie slapped the heel of her hand against her forehead. "You'll be the death of me yet, Devon Ritcey." She hugged her friend. "But it is brilliant, even if it is a bit dodgy."

"Okay, pizza," Harvey said, "this is getting cold." He turned and headed to the main room. "We can talk while we eat."

Natalie followed, looked back over her shoulder and shook her head. *Can we do this? Can we pull it off?*

In the main room, she accepted pizza on a paper towel and sank down on the sofa. *I'll decide once I eat.*

They were all on a third slice of pizza when Harvey asked the looming question. "How did this happen?"

Devon wiped her mouth. "First, I decided all the work you and Natalie did should *not* disappear. Hence the copies." She crumpled the paper towel. "I got the rest of the idea from you," she said, pointing to Harvey.

"Pardon?"

"You told me to call Mrs. Roberts and invite her for a 'visit.' Not for witness questioning, but for a visit to her old home." She tapped a finger against her temple. "My brain mulled things for a bit and asked me how we could turn the whole thing on its head."

"And you came up with an idea for a new investigation," Harvey said. "Good thinking."

Natalie licked sauce off her fingers. "But don't we need someone to ask us to look into Amara's disappearance?"

Devon tapped her fingertips together like an evil plotter. "No worries. It's all arranged." Leaning forward, she delivered her explanation. "We have a contract with Lenya to take the case." She sat back, obviously satisfied.

"She shouldn't have to pay," Natalie said.

Devon set her forefinger on the side of her nose. "The fee is one dollar, a whole loonie. She's happy to help, or should I say, she's happy to pay the fee."

Natalie eyed her friend. "Don't look so smug. I still have reservations about how this plays out legally. The contract is with the Security Agency - you, the guys, Kelsey and Jeff Brown are the employees. Harvey," she said, pointing a finger at him, "and I are still police officers and don't work for CCSA."

"Exactly. But you missed one person on the CCSA roster. Liam Brown, Jeff's brother, is on retainer for legal issues. This is where we need to dial in Greg and Sam. They've sorted it out with Liam. Finish up folks, we're off to Skype."

****

Fifteen minutes later, Natalie and crew were dialed in and facing Greg and Sam via the wonder of computers and screens. The pleasantries behind him, Greg started explaining his idea.

"First, we are licensed for security and private investigation work. Usually, we do security work. This case from Lenya is investigative. There's a lot of talking to people and weaving the stories together to make a picture of Amara's last day. You all know the drill."

Sam Logan continued. "Right now, we can't come to the island. Maybe in a week, we'll be back if things here in the UK go well. Jeff is on his honeymoon with Emily, and his expertise is the computer, not the face-to-face work. So Devon and Kelsey are left manning the office. Kelsey is an accountant, not an investigator. Devon is a photographer, but in spite of her crime scene background, she isn't an investigator either."

Natalie couldn't help commenting. "She sure can ask probing questions though and she gets answers."

Greg laughed. "True enough, but she needs help on this. You two are always bound by police conduct and conflict of interest concerns, suspension and vacation time included. Otherwise, I'd out and out hire you both. CCSA could use an investigative arm for jobs like this. However, there is nothing stopping you from hearing other stories about the past. And you can talk to Devon and help her put the picture together." He paused and looked at Sam.

"If you want to," Sam said, "you could do it unofficially and voluntarily. You, in effect, become witnesses to what other people know and say."

Harvey rocked back in his chair and rubbed his chin with two fingers. "It's convoluted, but still makes sense if I've followed you correctly."

Greg cleared his throat. "Harvey, you're on vacation, why don't you stay on site there, enjoy the ocean, the boats, meals at the café and time with Natalie." He mimicked his wife's finger-on-the-side-of-the-nose move.

Harvey saluted the two men on the screen. "Greg, my friend, I'll take you up on the offer," he said.

"And Natalie is here because we invite her to be for the same reasons," Devon added. "We'll all have tea and visit in the community and shop up at the grocery store. Maybe we'll get in some sailing. And I think Natalie would benefit from time with Adam and Mutt. Nothing like a crazy dog and a kid with a metal detector for some fun."

"It's settled," Sam said.

Greg named one last item. "We'll be in touch every day by Skype so you can update us. We have full confidence in you, but it is officially our case and our company, so we should go through the steps."

Natalie waved goodbye to Greg and Sam. "I'm back on the case, well the job at least. We'll get answers for Lenya as best we can."

Devon blew her husband a kiss and signed off. "What do you think?" she asked. "Can we make this work?"

Harvey leaned forward, arms on thighs and hands dangling between his knees. "I think so, and in doing so, we'll find out what happened to Gloria as well."

Devon stood and one hand on her midriff and the other fanning the air, waltzed around them. "See, I told you I had a plan." She twirled once more and perched on the desk.

"Well." Natalie drew out the word and pulled her mouth to one side. "I suppose."

"Suppose nothing," Devon said. "It's a good plan and you

know it."

Natalie burst out laughing. "Yes, it's a good plan."

Harvey looked at them. "If it works. We'll have to be careful and keep all details, record all 'talks,' and," he said, wiggling his eyebrows, "drink a lot of tea."

They all laughed.

Warm hope settled in Natalie's middle. *We'll get to the bottom of Amara's, and Gloria's, story, come high winds, high seas or pirates.*

****

Early the next morning, Natalie wrapped a throw around her shoulders and took her coffee out on the deck. Fog evaporated under hot sun and birds twittered in the woods. She stared at the green lawn leading to the first tree line. Behind the line of green sentinels, the old house and at least one grave slumbered, long forgotten. *Is there another grave?*

She warmed her hands on the mug and sipped slowly. Fact-by-fact the plan they'd devised rolled through her thoughts. They *could* talk to anyone they wanted. They *could* ask questions on Lenya's behalf. And they could report to Devon.

Remember to make your appointments. You need to see the neurologist and psychiatrist. Brayburn's stipulation can't be ignored.

The patio door slid open behind her and Harvey joined her, settling into the adjoining Adirondack chair. He raised his mug in greeting but didn't break the peace.

Natalie raised her mug in response and smiled. *We're good together. No need for idle chatter.*

When the sun dispersed the final fingers of fog, she spoke. "What time is Mrs. Roberts arriving?"

"In time for lunch. Vie has planned a salad meal for everybody."

Natalie rested her head. Birds, breeze and the odd boat motor took over the air waves. Calm and peaceful. *I missed this when I returned to work, to the city. I need to pay attention to my world.*

Harvey stirred and set down his mug. "Penny for your

thoughts."

She laughed. "Surely they are worth more these days. Inflation and all considered."

"True, so how about a loonie?"

"That's more like it." She drained the last dredges of coffee. "I'm contemplating my future. Looking at options and pros and cons." She indicated the scene before them with a wave. "This view is one I'd love to see each morning."

"It's a good one. Certainly, a pro when considering living spaces."

"Ah well, I'll see what transpires, both inside my head and around me. After, I'll make a decision." She turned toward him. "Although, leaving law enforcement is winning."

Harvey held out his hand and she took it. He squeezed gently. "Nat, whatever you decide, I'm behind you. I know I've said it before, but I truly mean it."

Natalie squeezed his hand. "Thanks, Harvey. Your support means the world to me. And I truly mean what I say." They grinned at each other like teenagers.

Harvey's touch, his grin and his words, coalesced around her. *Moments like this are what life is about. Amazing what holding hands can do to my insides.*

Harvey squeezed her hand once more and let go. He turned his wrist and checked the time. "Time for a shower," he said and levered off the chair. He took both their mugs. "Do you want more coffee?"

She shook her head. "I'd better get into action, too. We have a date with Mrs. Roberts for lunch." She stood beside Harvey. "I wonder what we'll learn."

****

At noon, Natalie and Harvey found Mrs. Roberts perched on a stool in the kitchen discussing recipes with Vie. Her white hair perfectly coiffed, her eyes bright and her pants suit a teal blue, she looked like a bird on a perch.

She beamed at them. "Harvey, nice to see you finally. And you must be Constable Parker."

Natalie put out her hand. "Natalie." The older woman shook

firmly. *Quite the grip for such a little woman.*

"And my name is Doris, not Mrs. Roberts."

Devon and Grace pushed through the swinging door. The six-year-old ran over and gave both Natalie and Harvey a hug.

Vie, drying her hands on her apron, turned from the sink and indicated the numerous dishes on the work island. "Okay everyone, grab a dish and let's move this do to the dining room."

Natalie picked up potato salad. "It's warm," she said. "Isn't potato salad usually cold?"

"It's the German version with warm baby potatoes," Vie said.

Natalie frowned. "Vie, you can't tell me you are German." She eyed the tall woman with mahogany skin and brown eyes.

The woman laughed and led the way to the dining room where china, silver, and crystal set the table.

"Oh my," Doris said, "I feel like royalty."

Devon added green salad to the meal. "I love to use the good dishes. This seemed the opportune time."

She seated Doris and the others found places. Soon the food was divvied up, and they were all enjoying the meal. There was even sliced meat for Harvey who enjoyed his protein.

The food disappeared and soon Devon wiped her mouth and laid aside her napkin. "Doris," she said, addressing the head of the table, "Amara's sister, Lenya, would like to visit with you. We'll go for tea."

Doris laughed. "Tea eh? Some things never change. But, I'd like to see Lenya. She was barely a teenager. I'm afraid she got shuffled off to the side during the whole mess. We have a lot to talk about."

She turned toward Harvey and Natalie. "And we have a lot to talk about as well." She winked at Harvey. "I understand you are interested in August 1969. I have quite the tale about that month." She rested her arms on the table. "You can ask questions if I'm not clear enough. I also brought Gloria's stash box for show and tell." She folded her napkin, matching the edges precisely.

Vie stood. "Come on, Grace, you can help me make the tea."

"We need four cups of tea," Grace said, "I counted while you were all talking."

"Thank you, Grace," Vie answered solemnly. "That's very

helpful."

Once they were gone, Doris Roberts started her recounting of the summer of 1969. "You know my husband moved us to Ottawa the year before?"

Natalie replied. "Yes, and that he wasn't happy about the friendship between Gloria and Amara."

Doris drew in a tremulous breath. "1969, August was hot and people were short-tempered. The hippies headed for Woodstock, the seniors stayed close to their air conditioners and the rest of us mopped our brows on a regular basis." Her eyelids fluttered, and her smile lines faded.

"Gloria was supposed to go to a camp, but I put her on the bus to Halifax. She missed Amara and had brooded all winter. For teenagers, friends are more important than parents." A sigh rippled through her. "Her dad didn't understand. When he found out she was here, I thought he'd have a stroke."

Natalie asked her first question. "Why do you think he was so adamant about separating Gloria and Amara?"

Mrs. Roberts folded her hands so tightly her knuckles showed white. Her lips pressed together and her jaw muscle jumped.

Natalie's antennae quivered. She'd touched a nerve there. She shot a look at Harvey, and he raised an eyebrow. He'd seen it, too.

"Howard was, how do I put it? A bit judgmental about many things." She sighed. "A bit paranoid actually. He was raised in a church sect with strict rules."

Natalie almost asked if he'd thought Amara was leading Gloria into bad ways. But she caught herself and waited. *Better not to lead a storyteller or a witness.*

"He fumed when he found they'd been going to the movies. He disapproved of them watching the boys' soccer team practice. And he outright forbade her to try out for the cheer leading squad." She realigned her napkin. "But the worst started when he saw Gloria and Amara walking arm in arm. It was nothing, but he was so suspicious." She slapped her hand on the table. Her next words were barely audible. "He thought they were, you know, gay."

Natalie sat back. Her earlier conclusion was bang on.

Tears ran down Mrs. Roberts' face. "I don't want to speak ill of the dead. Howard was a good man in his own way."

Harvey asked, "What did he do after he found out Gloria was

here?"

"I'd never seen him so furious." She cupped her cheek with a hand. "He slapped me and yelled terrible things. He threw clothes in a carry-all and grabbed his car keys."

Harvey stated the obvious. "He left for Caleb's Cove."

She nodded. "His last words to me were: don't you dare call and warn them, or so help me God, I'll kill you both."

What a thing to say. How far had Howard Roberts' fury driven him? "Do you think he meant it?" Natalie asked,

Doris shook her head. "He was prone to grand statements but all he'd ever done was hit one of us a few times. I thought I'd sent Gloria to safety." Folding her hands together, she pressed them against her mouth and stared straight ahead. Her hands came down. "I've blamed myself for not coming back with him. I might have saved her."

Natalie reached over and took Doris's hand in hers. *What a guilt for a mother to carry.* "You couldn't have known what he might do or how the girls would react."

Doris's wan smile touched Natalie's heart.

"Thank you," she said. "Will you find out what happened?"

Natalie nodded. "You bet we will."

Harvey pulled a toothpick from his pocket. "You can count on it." He tucked the pick into the corner of his mouth.

Natalie mentally shook her head. *He's thinking again. How would he function without those things?*

Mrs. Roberts looked up. "May I see where you found her? And can I give Gloria a decent burial once they're finished?"

"We can arrange it," Natalie said. *Even on suspension, I will make it happen.*

In the wake of those revelations, the kitchen door opened and Grace held it for Vie to come through with the tea tray.

"Let's go through to the sitting room," Grace said. "We'll be more comfortable there." Quite the little hostess.

"Sounds like a plan," Harvey said. He rose and gestured for the women to precede him.

Once seated, they talked about Vie's rose bushes, Natalie's sailing lessons, and Lem's tourist business. The ghost tours he guided brought hundreds to Caleb's Cove every summer. The graveyard, with the extra traffic, looked better than it had in decades and the café benefited from the tourists.

"But," Grace said seriously, "you do know the ghosts aren't real?"

The adults nodded.

"But Caleb was a real little boy," she added. "And the thieves made him fall to his death." She sighed and tsked in a perfect imitation of Mrs. Gerber.

Natalie laughed with the others. The curse Caleb's mother had supposedly put on the island laid the ground for numerous ghosts and stories. *I wonder if Gloria's ghost is hanging around.* In a novel, the two ghosts would be hanging out, waiting to be found. *But this is real life. All we have are bones and questions.*

****

Later, Vie and Grace headed to the kitchen, Devon and Doris went to tour the house and Nat and Harvey moved into the office.

Harvey carried Gloria's box. "The more we hear, the more I'm sure the girls were together right to the end the last day. What do you think?"

"I agree." Nat took the box and locked it in the desk. "What's next?"

Harvey dropped an arm around her shoulders. "I suppose a lit fireplace, good food and a bottle of wine are not what you're thinking."

Nat poked him. "You never know. However, plans regarding the case were more what I had in mind."

Harvey hugged her tighter and stepped away. "Oh darn."

"First, I'd like a walk on the beach. Walking and fresh air should shake our brains loose and help us see what to do next."

Harvey glanced out the window. "Nat, there's fog out there."

She laughed. "So, we need jackets. But we're not sugar and we're not salt, and as my mother would say, we won't melt."

Harvey threw up his hands in surrender. "Jackets it is. Let's go." He knew darn well he'd follow her anywhere in any weather. He walked behind her watching the sway of her hips.

CHAPTER TWELVE

"Race you." Natalie challenged Harvey and set off running the last stretch back to the cabin. He followed, simply keeping pace, until they arrived at Cabin Three out of breath and laughing.

"Thanks for going with me," she said. "I like a walk in the fog more than one in the sun. It is so insulated and calming."

"It shows on your face," Harvey said and taking her jacket hung his and hers on the rack. "You look more relaxed than when we started on our walk."

She shivered. "But the cool damp in here once I've stopped walking isn't as welcoming."

"I'll start the wood stove." Harvey knelt and adjusted the wood and paper. Striking a match, he set flame to the mix. He cupped his hands around the faint flare and coaxed it to life. Once the flame reached higher, he closed the door and watched through the glass.

"A fire should dry off the fog and warm us up. How about I make mac and cheese for supper?" He turned

Nat, curled on the sofa, stared at the flame, shaking.

Darn, I should have known the flames might trigger a flashback. He reached her and knelt until they were face to face. "Hey, look at me, not the flames." Putting a hand under her chin he gently lifted her head until her eyes focused on his. "Deep breath."

The fire snapped and crackled behind him, and she flinched. He didn't let her look at it. "Another breath. Now tell me what is in the corner, describe it."

"A wood stove. You started the logs burning. There is flame."

Harvey released her. "Good. Are there any explosives in the stove?"

"No."

"And therefore?"

"It's safe. It won't hurt us."

Harvey kissed her forehead. "How are you now?"

Nat drew a deep breath and forced out her words. "One, two, buckle my shoe."

Her shoulders dropped, and she unfolded her arms. He felt her tension flow out.

"And what about three, four?"

Her small laugh reassured him. "...close the door?"

"And what's the stove for?"

"Heat and light."

She smiled and raised a hand to his cheek.

A few more minutes and she'll have control. "And what about supper?"

"You're making mac and cheese."

"Right you are. And what kind of wine do we have?"

"Red," she said. "It's a Merlot. My favorite."

"And where are the glasses?"

"In the cabinet over the dishwasher." She cupped his face with both hands. "Thanks, Harvey. You sure know how to put a girl at ease." She lowered her hands.

Harvey brushed a hair strand back from her face. "Anytime, sweetheart, anytime." *And anything else you need, too.* He grinned. "If you're okay, I'm going to go and get the wine."

"Please. I'll be fine and I'd like a glass of wine."

He looked back from the kitchen. *When will reminders stop triggering her flashbacks?* He retrieved the wine and filled the glasses. Returning, he passed one to her. "Here's to solving this case."

Nat clinked her glass against his. "And to us, Harvey Conrad. I couldn't ask for better."

"Now," he said, "let's review the information and get specific about the questions we need to ask."

Nat sipped. "If, as Lenya said, Amara worked at the store, Mrs. Gerber will know when she left and when Howard Roberts came in. We can start with Mrs. G. and carry the time line forward from the encounter at the campground."

Harvey agreed. "She may also know who else was around." He settled squarely in his seat and put his heels up on the coffee table.

Nat matched his stance, sliding over to lean shoulder to shoulder with him. "Other details. Did anyone see Roberts' boat leaving for the mainland? Did he really call from Bridgewater? No caller ID on those phones. He could have called from anywhere. It's been a long time. Is Doris sure about the times?" She rested her head on his shoulder.

A comfortable way to spend time. The fire snapped but Nat didn't flinch. Harvey's stomach grumbled. *I hate to move, but I promised supper.* He shifted slightly and Nat sat up.

"I'd better get started on supper," he said and hitched forward ready to stand.

"I'll grate the cheese," Nat said. "You put the water on and start the roux for the sauce."

The conversation continued over the supper preparation. "If the girls planned to cross the sand flats at low tide, they'd have been on the island until then. We'll need the tide times."

Nat peeled plastic off the cheddar and started grating. "Devon mentioned high seas and gale-force winds from the New Brunswick storm. High wind and driving rain can cover any number of evil deeds."

They worked in tandem. Toasted French bread with garlic butter topped off the meal. "There we are," Harvey said and set the full plates on the counter. "Dig in."

Nat pulled a carton of molasses from the cabinet.

Molasses? What's she doing with it?

She opened the container and poured black, sticky liquid on the macaroni and cheese. Catching the last drip with a forefinger, she licked it off.

"You're going to eat molasses on your mac and cheese?" he asked. "Isn't that a little odd? I've never seen you do it before."

"I remembered to buy some molasses." She shook her head. "Not odd at all. I learned this from my dad. It's no worse than ketchup on eggs, or cranberries on turkey, or peanut butter on bacon sandwiches."

"Seriously?"

She forked up food and shoved it into her mouth, her eyes laughing at him.

"You never know about some people," he muttered. He reached for the molasses. "But I'm game. I'll try one mouthful."

Cautiously, he put one bite topped with the molasses into his mouth and chewed. "Hmmm, not too bad. But I think it's an acquired taste, one I'll leave for later."

Four mouthfuls later, Nat put down her fork. "I promised I'd take Adam to the old house tomorrow. He wants to try his metal detector up there."

Harvey finished his wine. "I have a thought. If Brayburn is shutting the first case down, we won't get FIS to help look for another grave. But Adam's detector is a good one. Dave didn't skimp." He broke off a chunk of his bread. "You know, it wouldn't hurt to do a full sweep ourselves."

Nat picked up the empty plates and, skirting the counter, headed for the dishwasher. "True." She yawned and stretched. "The fresh sea air is getting to me."

Harvey closed and started the dishwasher. *She looks like a satisfied cat.* He took her hand and led her back to the sofa and settled her. "How about herbal tea to finish the meal?"

She nodded and yawned again. "And then I may head for bed."

I could get behind that plan. Harvey turned away before his face gave away his thought.

Nat finished her tea, and stretching, yawned widely once again.

He removed the teacups, and came back and pulled her to her feet. She rocked toward him and he wrapped her in a bear hug. "A well-rested detective, or interviewer, is a sharp one. Get some sleep while you can."

She locked her arms around his girth and rested her head on his shoulder. "You're so practical." She yawned.

He pulled back, put a hand on her chin and tilted her face to plant a kiss. "Go on now. I'll be in the second bedroom if you need anything." He didn't outright say it, but he remembered nights when she'd fought nightmares and screamed in her sleep. More than once, he'd woken her, carried her to the sofa and soothed her with warm milk and cookies.

She kissed him back and turned toward her room. "Thanks, Harvey. Don't know how I'd manage without you." She laughed and, blowing him another kiss, stepped in and closed her bedroom door.

****

Natalie leaned against the kitchen counter and finished her morning coffee. Almost time to start working through her list for the day. First were talks with Mrs. Gerber and Lem and later a trip to the hillside with Adam and his metal detector. *Everyone talks eventually.* Her father's words resonated with her. Finding the right person to talk, or collecting details from numerous persons, would build a case. Her bones were telling her so.

The front door opened and Harvey came in dressed in his running gear. "Ah, you're up." He sniffed. "And I smell coffee. I'll be right with you."

She heard the shower run and, mere minutes later, the water went off. Harvey joined her, his hair still wet, and dressed in shorts and a tee shirt. She passed him the coffee she'd prepped for him.

He guzzled half the mug. "Who do we start with?"

Natalie put her empty mug in the dishwasher. "Lem. If I remember correctly, he's an early riser. He might have been only a teenager when the girls went missing, but old enough to remember details." She opened her phone and dialed Lem's number. After a short conversation she pocketed her phone.

"Lem's sorting more documents saved in the fire two years ago. He says he's happy to take a coffee break with us. I think we're supposed to bring the coffee," Natalie said. "We can pick up some at the café. Gwen will know how he takes it." They headed for the local museum.

Fifteen minutes later, they strolled along the boardwalk between the café and the museum, an old building housing the Cove's history. The arrival bell rang over the big double doors, announcing their arrival. Natalie glanced at the family tree charts on the left of the lobby. She focused on the Krause family tree, and the glaring empty lines under Amara's birthdate. *Such a heartbreaking sight.*

Lem appeared behind the reception counter, a sheaf of flyers in his hand. "Constables, you're looking casual today." He filled the holder on top of the heavy oak counter with brochures.

Natalie glanced down at her light skirt and tank top. "I suppose. You'd better call me Natalie. This is not police business."

Lem came around the counter, hugged her and shook hands with Harvey. "And I suppose today you're Harvey?" He raised one eyebrow.

Harvey inclined his head in agreement. "How are you, Lem?"

"As busy as usual. I thought I heard you two were shoulder deep in a case. What's with the time-off look?"

Natalie handed Lem his coffee and a muffin Gwen had included with the order. "Long story. The powers that be have wound up the case for now. The body we found is Gloria Roberts. We're," she said, clearing her throat, "on enforced vacation for various reasons."

Lem tipped his head. "Humph. No never mind as far as I'm concerned. What can I do for you today?"

"Lenya has hired Greg and Sam and the company to find out what happened to Amara. Devon is on the case, and we're chatting with people to help her out."

"If not official, I'd guess you're collecting history stories on the area," Lem said. He pointed to the benches tucked under the heavy staircase curving up to the second level. "Come on, let's visit."

Harvey pulled out his notebook and pen. "My memory is going," he said with a wink, "so I'm writing things down. Let's talk about the day Gloria and Amara went missing. I'm curious to find out what you remember."

Lem ran his hand over his mouth and dragged it down his chin. "The hot and heavy weather foretold at least rain. Dad put me to cutting the grass before the rain came." He paused to drink coffee. "I wasn't keen on the job. You've seen the yard. It's huge."

He sat with his eyes closed for several minutes. "There wasn't much breeze off the ocean late in the afternoon, and I stopped frequently for water. About one, Dad came home with fish and gutted them at the dock. Gulls screeched and fed on those innards."

The man has a memory for detail.

"Mom had closed the blinds in the house in the morning. She hung the laundry on the clothes line. Mostly sheets." He drew a deep breath and continued with his eyes still closed. "When I first went for the mower, a boat roared back around the north point and into the marina dock. I learned later it was Mr. Roberts coming back from the campground."

Lem opened his eyes. "I started mowing the back yard, the one between the house and the road. I'd finished there and in the side yard when Dad came out, ignored my progress and ran toward the driveway. I found it odd. Usually, Dad moved deliberately. He wasn't prone to running. Especially in the heat."

Natalie smiled. *Like father, like son.* "Do you remember the time?"

Lem answered immediately. "The sun started heading west, so about suppertime. I coulda' used a breeze landward off the water, but no luck."

Lem circled his forefinger and continued. "Okay, out on the harbor I saw three sailboats. I stopped mowing to knock the grass buildup off the blade. Not much sound except for those screeching gulls."

He held up one finger. "Then I heard a motor join the screeching. Easily seen, a rental boat headed out to the south point. Great fishing over there. Two guys with fishing rods stopped and dropped their hooks."

More possible witnesses—if we get their names. "Did you know them?"

"Couldn't really see them, but they wore baseball caps." He scratched his head. "But someone on the sailboats maybe got a closer look. Two were the rentals. Mr. Harris is long gone. However, I have some records and Wayne has more. Maybe we have the rental logs."

"And the third sailboat? Did you know it?"

"Sure. Only one person had a distinctive orange slash on the sail. Ron Curwood. Probably over for groceries or fishing bait."

"Anyone with him?" Harvey asked.

"As far as I could see, no."

Harvey scanned his notes. "So three sailboats and a motorboat to track down. Two sailboats and the motorboat were from the marina rentals." He looked at Lem who nodded. "Do you also have a box for 1969?" he asked. "Maybe photos from the campground, or beach parties, or any groups?"

"Hmmm," Lem said. "I might have. People turn in packets of

the things without looking through them. I get some surprising photos at times. I'll have a look."

Natalie hugged Lem. "Those are good leads. Maybe Mrs. Gerber can continue the story." She placed the back of her hand against her forehead. "Oh my, I think I need some cookies and tea." Harvey and Lem laughed.

She followed Harvey into the waning morning. "I'll take the car," she said. Reaching the car, she stopped. "Call me when you're done, and I'll come and get you."

"Good enough," Harvey said. "I'll check with Wayne about records his father might have left. It's a long shot, but no stone left unturned."

Natalie halted mid-step. "That's Curwood's car." She pointed at the low-slung black car sitting beside hers. She bit the inside of her lip. "Do you think he's keeping an eye on us? Or me at least?"

"Nat, relax. He's in for Gwen's home baking." Harvey chucked her on the shoulder. "However," he added, "I'll be vocal about how nice it is to be on vacation."

In spite of his assurances, annoyance trickled down Natalie's spine. "They need to leave me alone." She headed to her own car, her hope rising as she left the lot. Maybe they'd find Amara and close in on a killer yet.

****

Natalie pulled into Mrs. Gerber's driveway beside a car she recognized as Doris Roberts'. *If Mrs. Roberts is there, Mrs. Gerber knows about Gloria.*

Natalie looked through the open door. The two elderly women perched on chairs at the kitchen table. The one, an aunt who knew so much, the other, a mother with her reality recently altered. Two women left with scars from 1969. Instinctively they tipped toward the table, gaining proximity to each other.

Cups of tea, the community's panacea, sat in front of them and the teapot sat between them, resplendent with a brightly colored, knitted tea cozy. Hands worried teacups, and shoulders rounded in remembered grief. She'd arrived at a moment of silence. Nat took a huge breath and knocked. Waiting would not change a thing.

The women looked in her direction and each sat back slightly, severing their connection. Mrs. G. motioned to the extra chair. "Come, have some tea."

"I hear the girl you found is Gloria," she said, starting right in on the main issue. "And you and Constable Conrad are finished with the case." She sounded a bit judgmental.

"Now, Evelyn, I told you it wasn't their choice," Doris said, speaking up.

Evelyn Gerber sniffed. "Yes, I know. I don't understand the police sometimes. Shouldn't they find out what happened to Gloria? And Amara? We have a right to know. What are we going to do about it?"

Natalie patted her arm. "It's okay. What we are going to do is have some tea." She looked around the kitchen. "And cookies if you have some, and you and Doris are going to reminisce about August fifteenth, 1969." She winked. "And, as a FRIEND, I'm going to listen carefully, the way I listened to Doris, Lem, and Lenya."

Mrs. Gerber opened her mouth and snapped it closed. She stroked a forefinger through the air. "Got it. Now let me see, where shall I start?"

Natalie offered a prompt. "Amara Krause worked for you. Why not start there?"

Mrs. Gerber retrieved a cookie jar from the counter. "She worked hard and often asked for more hours." She placed cookies on a plate and returned to the table.

Natalie eyed the cookies and chose one. "Do you know why she wanted more work?"

"Saving money for university, she told me. She'd been accepted at Carleton University in Ottawa," Mrs. Gerber said, running her finger along a red stripe on the tablecloth.

"And she worked the day the girls were last seen?" Natalie asked.

"Stock day. I had her stocking the candy bins. We were alone in the store."

"Do you remember what happened?" Natalie asked.

"Couldn't forget it." Mrs. Gerber sighed. "I went over it in my mind so often afterward wondering if I could have done more."

Learning this part of the story could be crucial. "Why don't you tell me about it?"

"Amara came in for ten o'clock to help me with the stock. She had the candy boxes in the front aisle—the one along the big window—opening them. All of a sudden, she gasped and dropped the box cutter. She backed away from the window with her hand against her throat. Her face lost all color. Like a deer in the headlights, she was. She raced toward the back of the store and out the door."

"Did she say anything?"

"Actually, I thought her comment was strange at the time, although I understood it later. She said, 'Don't tell him I was here.' Curious, I went to look out. I didn't see anyone in front of the store, but up the street, Mr. Roberts was marching into the gas station."

"Did you see anyone else?"

"Not right then. I started to turn away and the station door slammed open, and Mr. Roberts come out. He headed toward me and started running."

Nat made a note or two. Everything Mrs. Gerber said lined up with Lenya's report.

"Behind him, I saw Lenya run around the building pushing her bike. She took a running start and headed the other way toward the campground like a bat out of hell."

"What happened when Mr. Roberts came into the store?"

"He stomped up and down the aisles and checked the storage and the walk-in freezer. He asked if I had seen the girls."

She looked a bit guilty. "He didn't ask if I knew where they were. Anyway, he left. I watched him go. He went south. Probably to check out the places the girls used to go. It would have taken him quite a while since he was on foot. It got busy then and I didn't see him again."

"How about later? Who else came in?"

"A family from the campground came in. I didn't know them." Mrs. Gerber shifted in her seat. "And Mr. Curwood came in for milk and bread like he did most days."

"And he was alone?" *What about the young Rey Curwood? Surely, if he'd been around, he'd have mentioned when the girls went missing.*

"Yes. His wife came sometimes, but she wasn't with him. And

their girl was at camp, I think. The son, Rey, he'd started working in Halifax with the police. Not sure if he was around or not."

CHAPTER THIRTEEN

"How about the girls? Did you see them again?"

Mrs. Gerber fidgeted. "I suppose it makes no difference now?" She glanced at Doris who nodded. "They came back later, in a panic. Gloria afraid her father would harm her, and Amara afraid for Gloria. I scooted them up to the apartment. I'd seen a bruise on Gloria's cheek more than once. Mr. Roberts had vicious temper, and I figured they'd be safe in the apartment."

Doris's mouth pinched in a straight line. "Like I told you yesterday, he did hit her, a few times. "For her own good," he said." Tears welled in her eyes. "I should have done something more." She fished a tissue out of her sweater sleeve and wiped her eyes.

Natalie looked back to Mrs. Gerber. "How long were they up there?"

"They were there when I closed up at six. I took them some sandwiches and drinks. They said they'd stay hidden somewhere until they figured out how to get safely off the island. By then Mr. Krause had raised a search for them."

"Do you know when they did leave?"

"When I came in the next morning at seven they were gone."

"Did they leave anything behind?"

Mrs. Gerber scooted forward and levered herself up. "Hold on a minute." She left the room and turned toward the bedrooms.

Natalie waited. What did the girls leave behind? Minutes later Mrs. Gerber returned. She handed Natalie a folded paper.

Natalie unfolded the brittle paper carefully. Written in pencil, the message had faded but could still be read.

Thanks, Mrs. G. It's dark, so we're leaving now. We'll stay hidden, you know where, until midnight and lowest tide and sneak across the flats. I'll send you a letter when we're safe and you can tell our parents. Hugs, Amara.

Natalie placed the page on the table. "This explains why everyone assumed the body on the beach was one of the girls."

Mrs. Gerber nodded. "I told the police how the girls planned to leave, but I never gave them the note."

"So the police knew you'd hidden them upstairs as well?"

Mrs. Gerber nodded.

"Did you tell anyone else?"

"It bothered me, Amara's parents worrying so. I went to see them a few days after the girls left, or I'd assumed they left. I told them what the girls planned to do, and promised I'd let them know when I heard anything. They went to the police who put out a watch. And the police talked to me."

Doris spoke up. "She called me, too, and, when they thought they were gone, Howard came home."

Natalie closed her notebook and helped herself to another cookie. "Thanks," she said. "What you did at the time made sense. At least now we know the girls were alive until well after dark. What did they mean by 'you know where?'"

"I assumed they meant the old house on the estate. But I don't know for sure."

Natalie's phone rang. After talking to Harvey, she rose to leave. "I have to go." Both women accompanied her to the door. She turned and waved goodbye. The women were huddled together, supporting each other.

Both harmed by remembering the shared past. I have to find out the truth. It's the least I can do for them.

****

Heading for the marina and café, Natalie wondered what Harvey had found out. Could they be lucky enough to find Mr. Harris' old records? She pulled into the lot, avoiding Curwood's car. *He's one heck of a slow eater. What is he up to?*

Before her car engine pinged into silence, her phone rang. Her eyes still on the black car, she answered.

Brayburn's voice blasted her ear. Always loud, this time he

topped the scales.

"What's going on down there?"

Natalie took a breath. Forcing all thoughts of 'Devon's case' from her mind, she provided as honest an answer as she could. "Not sure what you're referring to? But if it's my activities, I'm eating too many cookies, drinking enough tea to float my hind teeth and visiting with old friends."

"Humph. Mrs. Gerber and Mrs. Roberts I suppose," he said. "What is the dead girl's mother doing in Caleb's Cove?"

"You'd have to ask her, but I'd guess visiting old friends as well, sir," she said seriously. "And coming to grips all over again with her daughter's death. The news from FIS shocked her."

"For your sake, I hope you're telling me the truth," he said. "What were you and Conrad doing talking to Lem Ritcey?"

For that one, she crossed her fingers. "We were seeing if he needed a hand, since his assistant is still on her honeymoon." The honeymoon part was true.

"And did he?"

"Not today, so Harvey and I are going to take Adam Mason to a few new spots so he can use his metal detector. He's plucked about as much coin off the local beach as there is to be found."

"Really?"

Ignoring the sarcasm in his voice, she waited.

"Have you made appointments to see the medical team?"

Oops, I'd forgotten about that part. "I've been busy, sir," she answered. "I'll call them this afternoon."

"Good plan, Parker. I want to put this screw-up to rest and I want you to get sorted out."

"I guess we'll have to wait until we see the doctor's reports," she said. "You've made it very clear that my headaches, should they arise, are unacceptable."

Brayburn didn't like being bested by anyone. "Listen well, my girl, stay away from the Roberts case. We'll handle it in due time. And get those appointments, *tout suite.*" Her boss slammed down the phone, his frustrated vibrations echoing in her ear.

So, Curwood is keeping an eye on us. How else could Brayburn have learned what we are doing? Old boy network in action? Informing the chain of command. She sighed. *It is their job to know, but it's also annoying.*

The café doorbell jingled and Curwood exited the café. He paused and surveyed the entire parking area. Once in the car, he again looked toward her car. He obviously knew it. He peered out his windshield and seeing her in the car, raised a hand. She responded with a cheery wave and a wide smile. The man glared and left.

****

She found Harvey on the pier with Wayne Harris, who appeared to be showing him his fishing line.

Harvey looked up as she approached. "How about we go fishing one day this week?"

"You mean like we do every day?" She stuck her fingers in her front pockets and grinned. "Fishing for clues."

Harvey grinned back and glanced past her at the café. "How's our favorite official?"

"Gone. But he updated Brayburn before he left." She filled him in on the conversation. "They must be getting flak from the politicians or the news media."

"Most likely." Harvey shook hands with Wayne. "Thanks, when you call, tell Lem we'll follow up first thing in the morning."

"You bet." Wayne saluted. "Nice to see you, Natalie. You two take care now." And he walked off down the pier.

Natalie led the way back to the boardwalk and café. "Please tell me he knows where those records are?"

"He does. We may need luck given the time elapsed and the fire at the museum, but we'll know by tomorrow. He's going to let Lem know what to look for. It's a good thing for us Lem is fanatical about preserving documents." Harvey headed around the building. "Are we off to find Adam?"

"First some lunch." Natalie unlocked the car. "Then we'll go for Adam. I talked to Lydia earlier and she knows we're coming. Let's see if we can find signs of anything else hidden up there on the hill."

****

Adam perched on the bench in front of the grocery store, swinging his feet. Mutt lounged by his side. Both boy and beast hopped up when Natalie's car pulled in. More like lumbered up as far as Mutt went.

"We're ready," Adam announced. "I drew a grid. We can line up with the fallen tree and know where we are. I'll mark the spots on the grid where the detector finds things." He waggled his clipboard.

"You are prepared," Harvey said and opened the back door for Adam and Mutt. "I have a supply of marking pins and flags," he added, "so we can mark the spots on the ground. But remember, Adam. We probably need to leave the digging to the forensic anthropologist team."

"You bet," Adam said. "We don't want to mess things up, and I don't want to see any scary stuff."

"You two make good partners," Natalie said as she swung left at the Y junction and headed along Westerly Road. She pulled up at the now well-used spot. They pulled out their gear, including a lawn chair for Adam, and hiked up the old driveway until they reached the dig site.

"Wow, look at that." Adam circled the outside of the yellow tape. "What a big hole." He shivered. "And that's where the body was? For years?"

"That's right." Harvey set the lawn chair off to the side. "You should be able to see everything from here," he said to Adam and traded the metal detector for the lawn chair.

Adam looked back over his shoulder before settling in the chair. He consulted the sketch on the clip board and transformed to his old man persona. "Miss Natalie, if you put in the metal pins to mark the corners of the grid, we can get started. One row at a time. Let's work out from the bottom of that dug up area." He peered at the area stripped of grass and bush and dug into holes.

"What did they do there?" he asked, sidetracked.

"They dug up and sifted all the dirt around the perimeter of the grave," Natalie said.

"What were they looking for? Extra bits of bone?"

"That," she continued, "or buttons and things."

"Hmm." Adam tapped the pen against his chin. "Clever." He swung his feet. "Okay, start with the grids that are perpendicular to the first dig." He showed the sketch to Natalie. "If we find anything, we'll mark them with those little flags," he said.

"Yes, sir." Natalie saluted Adam. Harvey reported the grid number and turned on the metal detector. They progressed through the squares, moving slowly but steadily. Once they finished the first six squares, Natalie moved the pegs and, taking her turn with the detector, started back the other way.

They finished six more squares with no results. "Darn," said Adam, "I'd thought we'd find something pretty quick."

Natalie agreed with him. If they found nothing, they'd have to start over on Amara's disappearance.

Harvey reached out and ruffled Adam's hair. "Well, buddy, sometimes you do and sometimes you don't."

Mutt barked and rolled over exposing his other side to the sun. *Lazy. It's a wonder he found those other bones in the first place.*

She handed Harvey the detector, and he started scanning the square in front of Adam. The steady tick-tick escalated. "See. Something here for sure." He moved the instrument around until they'd identified a small area and Nat inserted a flag.

"Now we're getting somewhere," Adam said, swinging his legs faster. "Let's keep going."

Harvey laughed and moved on. Two squares went by with no more excitement but in the fourth square, the detector went crazy again. Harvey tested back and forth.

"The most activity is right there, by the bushes."

Natalie joined him. "Check into the middle," she suggested.

Harvey crouched and ran the detector around the bush, making two passes. Rapid, sharp beeps rewarded his efforts.

"This is a hot spot." He glanced at Natalie.

With her back to Adam, she raised her eyebrows. No telling what they'd find caught in the roots if they dug up the bush. After all, if the killer planted a young tree on Gloria's body, they might have done the same with Amara's and ended up with a bush.

The afternoon wore on and the sun passed mid-height and headed west. Several more spots triggered wild action. Mutt marked each activity with one sharp bark. After finishing the last square, Harvey and Natalie joined Adam in the shade.

"Time to cool off," Harvey said, "the sun is brutal today."

"But we've done good, haven't we?" Adam said. "We need to get them to dig again." He stilled his swinging legs. "Maybe they'll find another body?" His voice rose making his words a question.

"Time will tell," Harvey said. "We really don't know."

Natalie wiped the sweat off her brow. *But we sure can guess.* She lay back with one arm over her face. *Now we need to convince the FIS team to come back. Someone has to confirm a body, not only old metal. Harvey and I aren't in a position to relay this information. Time to talk to Devon.*

****

The others, as Harvey referred to them, consisted of Devon, Grace, and Vie.

Grace, lost in a huge apron and perched on a stool by the counter, helped Vie. "Hi, Adam," Grace said, holding up a sticky hand. "I'm making cookies."

Adam parked his metal detector and stood by Grace. "I love cookies," he said. "We found something," he told her.

Grace's eyes widened. "A body?"

"We'll see. We have to get the official people to dig it up."

"Devon nursed a cup and watched her daughter and Adam. "Sounds like you three have been busy." She gestured toward the stove. "There's tea on the hob if you're interested."

"Thanks." Natalie found mugs and got a quick affirmative nod from Harvey. "Two cups of tea it is." Life in the Cove included a workable knowledge of friends' kitchens. A unique experience harking back to the 'old days.'

"Milk and juice in the fridge," Devon said to Adam. "Help yourself." And he did.

Natalie jutted her chin toward the door. "Conference time," she said, leading the way.

Devon followed and Harvey brought up the rear as they headed for the office.

Devon settled on the desk edge and crossed her ankles. "Did your expedition turn up anything?"

"Certainly did," Natalie said and plunked herself down in a chair. "There's a lot of metal buried up there. What we found sure raises questions."

Harvey extracted the SD card from his camera. "Here," he said, "let's have a look on the larger screen." He handed the card over to Devon.

Turning on the computer, she brought up the grid pictures. The minutes passed as they scanned through the photos of the markers. The last picture, the numerous markers around and under the overgrown bush, made its appearance. "Most revealing," Devon said. "But what do we do about them?"

Natalie swiveled the chair. "We'll have to find a way to pass on this information. Right now, we can't." Even if they were right, their bosses might rain more wrath down on them for their actions.

"I could call," Devon said. "But how to explain how we got the information. Our methods are unorthodox at best."

Harvey uncrossed his ankles and pushed away from his favorite pose against the wall. "My thought is, we give it a day or two. Turner's coming to see us, and if I interpreted his cryptic conversation, he has information for us. With additional information, we may have enough to make a decision. Meanwhile, we can search the records Lem's looking for."

"Records on what?" Devon asked.

Natalie answered. "Information that Mr. Harris kept about his boat rentals."

"Holy crow, they're still around?"

"Yup. Lem encouraged everyone for years to pack up their files and photos and anything else and give them to him. He aims to make the museum unique."

"It's good for us," Harvey added. "We've found helpful information which led us to the paper work." He summarized Lem's statement. "Although the police asked if the girls had rented a boat, they had no reason to look further. Assuming the girls had run away would have had them looking in an entirely different direction. Now we are conducting a murder investigation. Quite a different species of fish."

He tugged his ear lobe. "The rental boat we need to check is the one with the two guys fishing. They'd be new witnesses and might have seen something."

"Did anyone else see the girls?" Devon asked.

"Yes. Mrs. Gerber did. With her information we can start to

see what they did that day. It's the same process as creating a current case," Natalie said. "Except harder to track down witnesses and to confirm what they remembered is correct."

"We do have an advantage," Harvey said. "We know the end game. The girls never left the island. What we need to find now, is what happened between six in the evening when Mrs. Gerber left them in the apartment and whenever they ended up dead. Since they planned to leave the island at low tide, which would have been sometime around midnight, there is a narrow window of time where they must have died."

"Six hours is still a big hole to fill," Devon said.

Natalie agreed. "But more manageable than a twenty-four hour window. Even if we find small pieces, we can begin to build a picture." She cocked her thumb and finger at Devon. "A picture of a killer." She fired her makeshift gun. "Bang."

****

Another damp night rolled through the Cove. Harvey, early to bed in the evening, crawled out of bed early the next morning. With blurry eyes, he peered at the clock. Not quite dawn and almost time to meet Turner.

He dragged on dark sweats and headed through the living room to the kitchen. The coffee, set on a timer, dripped invitingly into the pot. A door click alerted him to Nat's arrival. Like him, she wore dark trousers and shirt. And like always, she looked great, tousled hair, sleepy eyes and all.

He grinned at her and, threading his fingers through her hair on either side of her face, kissed her good morning.

She wrapped her arms around him. "I'm so sleepy. Did Turner have to come this early?"

"You know Turner. He checks his facts and rarely makes an unneeded move. Coffee?" He didn't wait for an answer before finding the mugs and pouring. He watched her face as she raised the mug to her mouth. As usual, her eyelids drifted closed, and she inhaled the aroma. He could get used to seeing her sleep-eyed look every day.

Fortified with coffee, Harvey and Nat stepped out on the back deck. Misty fog settled on their heads and shoulders. Calm air left the fog blanket thick over the landscape. Harvey took Nat's hand. "Off we go."

The grass, wet with mist, soaked through his sneakers. Fog brushing his face accelerated the waking up process. A faint swish and click penetrated the deadening effect of the fog. They quickened their pace, and the boathouse loomed over them. Their feet slapped on the boardwalk, and the dock beyond rocked under their steps. Moments later, a boat with two figures appeared and slid to a stop in front of him. *Turner and, wait a minute, a dog?*

Turner put a finger to his mouth signaling no talking and threw out the bow rope. Harvey caught it. Turner tossed the stern line to Nat before jumping to the dock. He turned back and with a two-finger swipe signaled the dog to join them. Using hand signals, Turner urged them up the dock and around the boathouse. Behind the boathouse, they ducked around a tree stand and stopped.

"Meet Bob," Turner said. "Bob, say hello."

The dog sat and extended one paw to Nat.

"He has good manners," Harvey said. "He knows to shake with the ladies first." He shook the paw now offered to him. "Why did you bring the dog?" he asked.

"Retired police dog. Special skills," Turner answered. "Come," he said, directing the dog. "Let's go further up the hill. Can't have our voices carrying over the water." He smiled, his teeth a white slash in his dark skin and led the way.

The chilly procession climbed without comment, their ascent marked by the occasional clink of the dog's tags. They gained the wooded area and the bushes, wet from the fog, added moisture to their clothing.

At the old house, Turner stopped. Bob sat behind him.

"Now," Turner said. "First, rules of engagement. Bob and I are figments of your imagination. Got it?"

Harvey and Nat nodded.

"Second, Bob's nose is a finely tuned instrument. He's found remains buried for decades and identified spaces where bodies were previously buried. If he didn't have a dodgy ticker, he'd still be working.

"Third, the old file you wanted came through."

"And you read it?"

Turner looked at him, his steady gaze a reference to the silliness of Harvey's question. "What do you want first?"

Nat, standing beside Harvey, shivered. "Why don't we put Bob to work first? And after we're finished, go down to my place where it's warm to do the talking."

"As you wish." Turner knelt beside Bob and scratched his ears. "Ready to go back to work, old boy?" Bob wiggled. Turner fastened a wide, soft collar around the dog's neck. "Bob, search," he ordered, and the dog started a zig-zag search, his nose to the ground. Soon he barked one sharp woof. He'd found the now empty grave. Turner rewarded him with a treat. "Find it," Turner said and pointed with his left hand.

The dog moved forward again and in moments stopped. He took two extra sniffs and lay down, his head between his paws and nose pointing at the base of the bush they'd identified earlier.

"Good dog, well done." Turner scratched Bob's ears and gave him two treats.

"Where did you get him?" Nat asked. "It's not like there are retired cadaver dogs lying around."

"He's mine," Turner said. "Adopted him when they retired him."

How long have I worked with this man and didn't know about the dog? Harvey looked at Turner with a new respect.

"I take it those markers have a purpose?" Turner said, still kneeling by the dog.

"We used Adam's metal detector and identified buried metal."

"Good enough," Turner said. "Your second grave is now marked in two ways." He stroked Bob's ears. "How will you secure this?"

Harvey snorted. *Leave it to Turner to ask the salient questions.*

"Given my suspension," Natalie said, "I can hardly call the detachment for a surveillance team."

And my vacation means I'm not supposed to be following up on this site. We're darn lucky the killer hasn't been back already. After all, he, or she, will know where the second grave lies."

Turner scratched Bob's ears once more and stood. "I could..."

"NO," Nat answered in sync with Harvey. He gave her a high five.

"There's no point in getting you suspended, too," Harvey said.

"But thanks for the offer."

"Through the day," Natalie said, "anyone headed up here would be seen. You can bet the whole community is watching everyone."

She had a point. Nighttime might be different. "We could assume that if they wanted to come back, they would have done so already. Or we find a way to watch the grave."

Harvey looked at Nat who turned to Turner. "Risky to leave it totally unattended," he said. "Let's head inside and figure this out over coffee. There's enough daylight now to discourage any major disruption here."

****

At the cabin, Harvey set out water for Bob and coffee for the three humans. He stood in the kitchen, facing Turner and Nat across the work island. Bob lay in front of the sofa, satisfied with his morning's work.

"Who can you trust to help surveil the place?" Turner asked.

"Lem, Devon, and Jackson," Harvey said. "And Lydia Mason at the grocery. They can cover the road leading to the site."

"Devon can lock the main gate to the estate," Nat added. "And turn on the sensors and alarms for the house and boathouse. She's had them off with all the comings and goings."

"Our best defense is not breathing a word about the second grave." Harvey raised his mug in salute. "We have a short window to nail down the rest of this. Now, Turner, what do you have for us?"

Turner raised one shoulder. "The old file doesn't help. Bad news, a clumsy viewer tipped coffee or tea over it and two pages are obliterated. Crucial information is so blurred the human eye can't read it."

Blast. "I assume you have good news as well." Harvey had partnered with Turner long enough to know his patterns.

Turner set down his cup. "Maybe. The officer who found the body is listed as Constable Patsy Creaser. Isn't she related to you somehow?"

"That she is." Harvey's hopes rose. "She's my father's second cousin and she was the first female officer in the district. She's retired now, but I know exactly where to find her."

Turner stood. "I trust our visit helps. If I can help further, just ask."

"Thanks, Turner. I appreciate it."

"You'd do the same for me." He snapped his fingers at Bob. "Now we need to be on our way before people are out and about. I have a fishing rod, so it'll look like I'm fishing."

Harvey walked him to the patio doors. "Do you really fish?"

Turner grinned at him. "Only for clues," he said. "My stint in the navy was as an underwater technician. I feel exposed on the surface."

"Well, I'll be damned. I never even knew you were in the navy."

"It was a lifetime ago." Turner pushed open the door. "And there's a lot you don't know about me." Bob trotted out and Turner followed him. He raised a hand in farewell and disappeared toward the dock.

Harvey watched Turner's dark-clad figure stride across the lawn with the lanky dog at his heels. Turner had been correct about the 'retired officer' being as silent as a mime. Bob was as quiet as they came.

CHAPTER FOURTEEN

Behind Harvey, pans clattered and he turned to see Nat putting a frying pan on the stove. The egg carton sat on the counter with a pound of bacon beside it.

"Good downhome breakfast?" he asked and pulled out the toaster and bread. "Count me in."

Later, he patted his middle. "Ah, now my brain is working. Excellent breakfast, sweetie."

"Thanks and back at you." Nat washed down the last of her toast and yawned. "This may be a long day."

No doubt. He had Patsy to track down, and with any luck, more witnesses to interview. If Lem found the marina records, they'd have those to sort through as well. His phone rang and the museum ID appeared.

"Good morning, Lem," he said. "What's the news this morning?"

"Found the records you wanted in a set of bankers' boxes. There are a lot of them, but I've identified three belonging to 1969. They look jumbled, but if you're lucky, you'll find something helpful."

"I'm delighted," Harvey said. "To tell you the truth, I doubted you'd find them. What is it about this place? The entire population hoards paper and photos."

"Simple," Lem said, "I trained them. History is important. One never knows what tiny fact will make sense of someone's heritage, or," he paused, "lead to a treasure or an old whiskey cache."

"In our case, we'll settle for clues to our case." Harvey glanced at the clock. "I'll be along pretty quick for the boxes. You'll be there?"

"Yup," Lem answered and hung up the phone.

Half an hour later, Harvey and Nat hauled three boxes into the kitchen. Digging into them, they sorted and stacked paper. Accounting ledgers for gas sales went in one stack, order copies for confectionaries and fish bait in another. Invoices and receipts for the expansion into a café made up the third.

Harvey flipped through documents stapled at the spine. "He certainly kept detailed records for the construction. Let's hope the habit carried over to the boat rentals."

Nat removed the lid from the third box. "Last chance. Cross your fingers." She lifted out five-and-a-half by four-inch ledgers. "Before the bridges were built in 1978, people could only get here across the flats at low tide or use boats. Looks like Mr. Harris rented rowboats, powerboats, and sailboats. And look at these records. I think I love this man."

"Even if people could get across the flats, low tide occurred only twice every twenty-four hours," Harvey said and picked up a ledger. "I'll bet his docks and boats were in big demand."

Nat retrieved the next binder. "We're looking for small motorboats rented the day the girls went missing. Lem didn't see them disappear to the south. But if they'd gone across to the north, the space is wide enough he'd have had time to see them go."

Harvey surveyed their stacks. "Paper work, in combination with phone calls and stakeouts, makes up the boring side of police work." He leaned against the counter and started checking dates. "This one is June and July," he said and tossed it aside. Before he could reach for another one, Nat spoke up. "I've got August."

Harvey rounded the counter, and put a hand on the ledge and one around Nat's shoulders, and started reading. "Caution must have been Mr. Harris's middle name. Look at those columns. Date, time, renter, ID like a driver's registration number, and time returned. And this line recorded the boat, motor and life jackets' condition."

Nat pointed. "And a signature from the renter agreeing Harris reviewed the safety issues and supplied life jackets."

Harvey peered closer. "Looks like he wanted to be sure he got his property back and didn't get sued. Where are the entries for our target date?"

Nat flipped pages until she came to August fifteenth. "Bingo.

Look here. There are some early morning rentals, but these guys rented a boat and motor late afternoon. There's only the one entry." She tapped the spot and dragged her finger across the bottom of the entry. "Here's a driver's ID number for a Matt. I can't make out the second renter's initials. Might be BL or RF."

She turned the faded writing toward the light. "And look here. There's a note on the next line documenting when the boat was returned." She poked the page. "They returned it mid-morning the next day. Harris charged them extra for overnight."

"Gone all night. This may be the break we need." Harvey chucked Nat's shoulder. "If we can track them down, we may have a witness who actually saw something useful."

She looked at him through squinted eyes. "Maybe," she said, drawing out the word. "They even did something."

She had a point. Harvey pulled out his phone, focused on the screen, and snapped a picture. After confirming it came out clearly, he sent it to Turner. *Maybe one of these two is the killer or our link to the killer. At the least, they may have crucial information.*

They sorted the other forms but found nothing else relating to the fifteenth or sixteenth of August 1969. Nat made new information cards to go to the evidence board and they headed for the office.

Turner called about half an hour later and Harvey put him on speaker. "Good news," he said. "Matt Mackenzie is still in the system. He lives in Chester," he told them. "He's semi-retired and had several DUIs. If not at home, he can be found at the *Fo'c'sle Pub and Bar* for supper and beer. Apparently, it's walking distance from his house. A necessary situation because he's currently without a driver's license."

"Thanks, Turner." Harvey hung up and held out a hand to Nat. "So, who talks to whom?" Harvey asked.

She linked her fingers with his. "Why don't you go and see your cousin, Patsy. I'll take this Matt Mackenzie."

Harvey kissed her on the forehead. "You be careful."

"Back at you," she said and turned to leave.

****

Although she had a yen for high speed, Natalie drove within the speed limit. The rising assurance they were on the right track sharpened her awareness. She tapped her fingers on the steering wheel in time to the music. *I can smell the end of this hunt.* With luck, the new witness had answers, clues to what happened. All she had to do was get him to spit them out. A glitch shot through her rising energy. *Will the information reveal Mr. Roberts as the killer? If so, how will Doris Roberts react?*

Resting on the ocean edging the secondary road, boats and buoys reflected in the still water. Late afternoon heat shimmered off the pavement. The utter stillness foretold a coming storm. She drove through another picturesque village and rolled into Mahone Bay. After passing the three famous churches, she made a right turn around the inlet and headed toward her destination.

Chester's maze of streets welcomed her and the GPS guided her to Matt Mackenzie's house. Her dashboard clock marked five as she parked in front of a small wooden bungalow. Unlike its neighbors, it sorely lacked upkeep. The uneven flagstones provided tripping options. Avoiding, them, she headed for the veranda which stairs needed staining. Bracketing the steps, the fancy posts holding up the roof could use new paint.

A lion's head knocker hung on the door. She raised it and rapped three times. Time ticked by. *Is he up at the pub?* She turned and looked up the street. *One more try on the knocker.* But the lock grated open and a crack appeared between door and frame, revealing a face. *Heavy eyes, scruffy chin, and weathered skin. This man looks older than his sixty-seven years.*

"What do you want?" The raspy voice matched his appearance.

"I'm looking for some information." *Is my lack of badge good or bad with this dude?* "We know you spent time out at Caleb's Cove in 1969. We thought you might have some information we need."

"Probably not. 1969 is ancient history, and my brain is a bit fuzzy these days."

Probably has to do with the beer fumes radiating off you.

"I'd like to talk to you, anyway," she said. "It won't take long, but we'd be more comfortable inside."

The man drew a breath and held it. Finally, he moved back,

and the door swung slowly open. Natalie stepped in. Old beer, left-over pizza, and unwashed man odors filled the space. She sucked air through her teeth and held her breath.

Matt Mackenzie led the way into an equally dark and stale living room. The beer bottles and stacked pizza boxes confirmed her assessment of the odors. Matt settled in a recliner between the table holding the beer bottles and the pizza boxes stacked on the floor. He didn't invite her to sit.

She inspected the orange, brown and beige sofa and its outdated floral pattern. Dingy lace curtains screamed of decades hanging in a smoke-filled room. A matching chair across the room faced Mackenzie's recliner. She sat, gaining a face-on view of Matt but removing her from smelling range. She allowed the minutes to tick by and watched him shift in the chair, take a swig from a part-full beer bottle and finally acknowledge her presence.

She began her questions, keeping a sharp watch on the man's face. "Have you seen the news item about the body found in Caleb's Cove?"

He inclined his head. "Hard not to. What's that got to do with anything?"

"Obviously, the police are investigating the situation."

"Ya. Are you the police?"

Tricky question. "I've been hired in a private capacity to help find the girl's friend."

He sneered. "You talk like a cop."

"I'm an investigator."

Matt grunted and let it go.

Natalie pressed forward. "In looking at old records, we discovered you were in the area the day the girls went missing."

"You mean when they drowned." He swigged back more beer. "Coulda' been. What's it to ya?"

So he does remember. And he's made a point of mentioning drowning. What does that tell me?

She pulled out her notebook and flipped it open. "You left your driver's ID at the boat rental late in the afternoon. You and a friend spent time fishing at the south point. Then you moved on and didn't return the boat until mid-morning the next day."

"If you already know it, why come bother me?"

"We're interviewing anyone who might have seen something," Natalie said and turned to a blank page. "So it's obvious you're on our list."

"Not to me, it isn't." *Surly is as surly does. This man isn't going to be helpful. But for what reason? He doesn't know anything? Or he doesn't want to talk?*

Natalie's phone rang before she could ask her next question. She looked at the caller ID. *Harvey.* After two more rings, she answered. "Parker."

"Are you at Mackenzie's house?"

"Yes."

"I found Patsy. We had quite a chat. She remembered the case well. First time she'd found a body. There are numerous details you'll want to hear, but the bottom line is the man's identification, the one who confirmed Gloria as the deceased. At the time, he said he remembered Gloria wearing a silver chain with a medallion he could identify. Brace yourself, Nat. The young man was none other than Rey Curwood."

Wow. Natalie dropped her pen. "Really? Interesting." *Man, interesting indeed, and then some.* She retrieved the pen, hiding her face for the time it took her to reclaim neutrality.

"Not nearly as interesting as his middle name. Our esteemed leader is none other than Rey Jarvis Curwood."

R.J. Nat wrote it down. Not BT or BL but R.J. None other than her boss's boss, a well-respected and decorated police officer who had joined the force in 1969. How was he involved? The knot in her stomach tied another loop. Why hadn't he mentioned he'd been in the Cove the day the girls went missing? And why identify the corpse from the beach as Gloria Roberts?

Is this one of those: 'do-the-right-thing-no-matter-what' times?

"Nat, are you still there?" Harvey's voice pulled her back to her task. She glanced over at Mackenzie, but he was busy picking the label off his beer bottle.

"Yes, ah um, I do see. Good to know," she said, as calmly as she could. "I'll seek additional confirmation."

"Hope you nail it," Harvey added. "If Curwood was involved, we not only need our ducks in the proverbial row, we need them harnessed and shackled and unable to fly."

A muscle twitched in Natalie's jaw. Resolve slid down her spine. Harvey was right. If Curwood was involved in the murder, she'd need nails by the pound to secure his coffin. Getting past Brayburn alone would take some doing. Especially since she wasn't supposed to be anywhere near the case. "Will do."

"I'm on my way. You may not need backup, but my gut is telling me we've found the key to the puzzle and I want in on the action. Take care."

Natalie set her phone on the dusty side table. "Now, Mr. Mackenzie, where were we? Oh yes, you were about to outline your time, detail by detail, from the instant your boat went around the south point until you returned to the boat rental outlet."

He upended the beer bottle against his lips and swallowed twice, emptying the bottle. Setting it on the table, he burped loud and long. "Nothing to tell. We fished, we put to shore and drank some more, fell asleep and came back in the morning." He burped again. "I was some stiff, I'll tell you." He arched his back and raised his shoulders.

Natalie leveled a stare, narrowing her eyes slightly.

Mackenzie pinched his lips together and tilted his head side-to-side before rolling it down on his chest. She could almost hear the nah-nah, ah, nah-nah accompanying the move. But she had an ace up her sleeve. Two summers previous, she and Jeff Brown had sailed the shoreline in question looking for drug runners and their potential landing spots. *Mackenzie is lying.*

"I'm a bit confused," she said, "I know that area quite well and all I remember is high cliffs and rocky areas. Can't think of a spot where you could pull ashore like you say." She put on her thinking face, her lips pressed together and twisted to one side. "Rock doesn't change in fifty-some years." She paused again. "Unless you put in at the dock for the estate."

Mackenzie shifted and looked out the window. "Let me think." He lined up the bottles on his coffee table, used his cuff to wipe up a spill and brought his attention back to the conversation. "We might have used the dock. Too long ago for my memory. And we had drunk a lot. Too much booze gives me blackouts."

"You were, what, twenty-one? Legal drinking age and a bit old for sneaking off to get drunk."

"No limit on getting away with a bottle," Mackenzie said and, plucking a crumpled tissue off the table, swiped it across his nose. "But if you must know, it was a farewell trip."

Natalie waited, tapping her pen on the notebook.

"R.J. had graduated and started his job. I needed one final year at Mt. Allison."

Step one, he's mentioned R.J. Natalie tamped down her rising anticipation.

"We'd decided to re-visit our youth, well, our earlier youth. No big deal."

Natalie drew a line on the open page. She didn't want to put too much emphasis on her next question. "And who exactly is R.J.?"

For the first time, Mackenzie tensed. He scratched his forehead, letting his arm partially cover his face. "Just a guy I knew." He dropped his hand onto the chair arm and flicked at a spot she couldn't see, giving it his undivided attention.

"If you knew him well enough to take this nostalgic drinking trip, you must know his full name." She couldn't prompt him, he had to tell it on his own, in case the remaining story explained two murders. "We need to question this person as well. If what you say is the truth, he'll be able to confirm it."

"I can't."

"Can't what? Remember the name? Or can't tell me what it is?"

Sweat glistened on the man's forehead. "Look, nothing happened. But I can't tell you his name."

Natalie leaned forward. "If nothing happened, what's the problem?" She pointed her pen at him. "Sounds suspicious to me."

Mackenzie launched off the chair. "Leave it alone." He turned and headed to the hall. "I need another beer." He disappeared into the kitchen.

Natalie stood and cocked her head. The fridge door opened and a bottle top popped.

Do I follow and confront him? Take his beer away? Or should I threaten to take him to the police? What will shock this man into telling the rest of the story?

She met Mackenzie in the arch between living room and kitchen. Wrapping her hand around the bottle neck, she pried it from his fingers. "You need to tell me what happened. But if you don't want to talk to me, I can call the Bridgewater police and tell them you have information about the day the girl died. And they'll forward the information to the senior officer in Halifax named Curwood. He has all the files."

She'd never seen a man buckle at the knees before. It happened so fast she couldn't stop his descent. Down on his knees, hands over his face, he rocked back and forth, moaning.

Natalie put down the beer and crouched beside him. "What's wrong?" *Oh heavens, did I trigger a heart attack or stroke in the man*? "Can you get up?"

He rocked and moaned.

She grabbed one shoulder and shook him. "Mr. Mackenzie, get up."

The direct command got through to him, and he stopped rocking. Putting one hand against the wall he struggled to his feet, following Natalie up as she stood.

She helped him back to his chair and went to the kitchen for water. He gulped down the drink.

He spluttered. "Nasty stuff," he said and handed her the glass. "Police cruelty to have me drink water."

"You'll live." Natalie went toe-to-toe with him and put her hands on her hips. "Now, what caused that collapse?"

He shook his head. "Nothing."

"Mackenzie, you are a terrible liar. We both know you have a story about that day. It's been over forty years. Don't you think it's time you told it?"

"No one will believe me. He said so. I'll go to jail and he won't."

"Who?"

The man's shoulder slumped, and he stared at his lap. He answered, but she'd couldn't make it out.

"Say again. A little louder, please."

"R.J. Curwood, the cold-hearted bastard. He'll bury me."

Exhilaration flooded her and anticipation zinged over her skin. *She drew in and held a breath. Never do to show my excitement.*

"Thank you," she managed. "I'm talking to you now, not Curwood." *Need to stay calm.* "You have the first chance to tell what happened. Your story will be the basis the others are measured against. If you are telling the truth, we'll do our part to prove your side. Will you talk?"

It was as if breath, air and time halted for long seconds. Please spit it all out. Tell me what I think you're going to tell me.

Tears ran down the man's face. "I can't take it anymore. Jail wouldn't be any worse than living like this. What do you want to know?"

Natalie released her breath slowly, steadily, using it to rein in her thrill. She couldn't risk having Mackenzie change his mind. *How best to handle it?*

He lifted his head, his pupils dilated. "Will you tell Curwood?" Fear laced his words.

There's my cue. Keep him calm. Help him know and believe he is safe from Curwood.

"No, I promise you we're not going anywhere near Curwood until we have the full story, the facts, and the evidence. We won't even talk to him until we can put him in custody." *For questioning at least.* The rest of Mackenzie's story would determine what they did with and to Curwood.

Mackenzie didn't seem to notice she'd reverted to talking like a police officer. He started rocking again. "He'll kill me, I know he will. He has a temper, keeps it under wraps, but it is there. Never mind the temper, he has contacts, people who will do his bidding for favors."

What other secrets might rest in Curwood's Pandora's Box? And what is he doing to the records he took away? Thank goodness Devon make copies."

"We'll stop him. He won't get to you." *I wish I felt as sure as I sounded. So much depends on how much Mackenzie tells me.*

Mackenzie looked up at her as if he didn't believe her. "If I tell you, I'll end up jail. And maybe Curwood, too. He'd get to me there."

The story sounded worse with each additional detail. Time to halt the recitation until she could record it with another officer present.

I want to hear it all. Hurry up, Harvey.

"Your statement will go a long way to influencing your outcome," she said. "I'm going to call a friend on the Bridgewater detachment. We'll record your statement here. We won't take you anywhere that Curwood will find you."

The man sighed and struggled to his feet. "Do what you can. I've kept this secret too long." He waved a hand at the beer bottles. "And look what it's done to me."

Natalie initiated the call to Harvey and followed Mackenzie who was heading for an already opened beer.

Natalie cut him off and whipped the bottle away. "Coffee time," she said. "We need you sober."

CHAPTER FIFTEEN

Harvey tapped his Bluetooth for the incoming call.

"Harvey, where are you?" *Nat.*

"Almost to Chester. What's your address?"

Nat gave it to him. "He's willing to talk. I'm going to pour some coffee into him and when you get here, we'll get his statement."

"Was he involved in the death?"

"Yes."

"And R.J?"

"Also yes, at least peripherally."

Surprise, surprise people and the other shoe drops. Harvey leaned forward and checked the dashboard clock. "I'm thirty minutes out. I'll try to make it faster. Hang on."

Harvey shifted in his seat, gripped the wheel with both hands and stepped on the gas. He needed to get Chester pronto. The speed needle rested above the legal limit but he didn't back off.

Nat's call confirmed what his gut had told him when he got the information from Patsy Creaser. A senior, well-respected officer was involved in a serious crime. And they were about to find out just how involved.

In the end, whatever they exposed him for could put an end to both their careers. There still existed a few officers who lived by the code of covering for your brothers in uniform. But would any officer back a murderer? Either way, the backlash could be brutal.

The street sign appeared behind tree leaves and he turned onto Mackenzie's street. Two blocks in, he eased in behind Nat's car and shut off the ignition. He slapped his own chest. *Here we go.* Grabbing the recorder, he exited the car and strode up walk. He hesitated on the porch, checking the area, before knocking. *And what waits behind door number two?*

Nat opened the door. The grin on her face lit the space, no doubt about it. *She's as energized as I am.* "How are you?"

She huffed and tipped her head. "Hard to say. Partly excited, partly terrified. Not sure what exactly we're going to hear or what we'll do with it once we do. You?"

He closed the door behind them and they lingered in the foyer. "That sums it up. I don't think there can be a bigger, scarier case than one involving a fellow officer. I've never been in this situation before."

"I hear you. This is a first for me. Are you ready?"

"As I'll ever be." Harvey put out a hand, ushering her into the hall and through to the living room.

"You do the interview," she said, before leading him to the kitchen. "I've already questioned him and might inadvertently lead his answers. If ever there was a time to avoid that, this is it."

Harvey nodded, and recorder in one hand, entered the kitchen.

Used dishes filled the sink. The garbage can yawned open, the lid resting on surplus trash. Mackenzie, his head in his hands, sat at the table. *Dejected sums up both the man and his home.*

"Mr. Mackenzie, Matt," Nat said. "This is Constable Harvey Conrad from the Bridgewater Detachment. He'll take your statement and record it. Just so you know, I'll also take notes".

Mackenzie lifted his head from his hands and looked Harvey up and down. "Whatever, let's get this over with."

Harvey sat beside Nat and across from Mackenzie. His chair creaked. The table wobbled. Turning on the recorder, he dictated the usual preamble. He launched into the interview.

"Mr. Mackenzie, in regard to August fifteenth and sixteenth, 1969, we'd like to hear your information."

Mackenzie sneered, a small taint of his bravado from earlier clinging to him. "You mean ya wanta know what the hell happened, eh?"

"Yes, please, sir."

Where do ya want me to start?"

Harvey shot Nat a look.

"Please start with leaving the fishing area. You know what you told me before? You need to tell Constable Conrad."

Mackenzie again reiterated the fishing and drinking reasons he and R.J. were out on the water. He stated how many fish they caught. None. How they finally went down the coast and pulled in at the dock for the estate.

"We knew Bockner and his people were gone and the full-time caretaker, Mr. Roberts, had quit his job and left. A local man looked in on the place, but no one lived on site. The previous two summers, we'd used the caretaker's vacated house to party during bad weather."

"And the weather that day?"

"At first, the weather was great and we fished, but when the wind came we put in at the dock. And when it started raining, we went up to the house. We had some chips, pop and jerky and a twenty-sixer of rum plus twenty-four beer. We were going to leave at one point, but the storm made it too risky to take the boat out, so we decided to stay. We settled in the front room at the house and kept drinking. Man, talk about blitzed. Curwood always could hold his booze better than me, but that night he'd topped his limit."

He stopped and drank coffee. "Bah, nasty stuff, coffee." He toyed with the mug and resumed his story.

"I passed out or went to sleep, whatever. I woke suddenly and there were voices in the kitchen. It took me a bit to shake off sleep before I stumbled out to have a look." More coffee followed by a shudder. "I found Curwood with two girls."

They needed complete details and Harvey inserted a question. "Did you know the girls?"

"Sort of. They'd been to the beach parties over the past couple of years. And we knew who they were."

"Can you tell us their names?"

"Amara Krause and Gloria Roberts—as if I could ever forget. They were both pretty but Gloria, what a looker. Stacked. Most of the guys tried to cozy up to her. But she'd laugh and tell them they didn't want to get involved with jail bait."

Mackenzie fidgeted. Looked like his fuzzy brain had made a solid connection between their visit to him and the girl's death. But as he'd said, he was ready to get it off his chest. How many cases were solved when some other suspect wanted to do just that?

Mackenzie appeared to have drifted into his thoughts without opening his mouth. "What about Curwood?" Harvey asked.

"Oh, he tried. He had the hots for her. He'd promised her he'd nail her one day. He was so sure of himself, so full of how good he was, he just knew she'd come around."

Harvey kept his voice level and his questions factual. "And did she ever indicate she'd be interested?"

"No way. She brushed him off like the others. And if he tried to get her alone, the other one would show up and take her back to the fire."

Did the two men clue in that the girls were gay? He glanced over at Nat. She had a question mark beside the same information in her notes.

Mackenzie folded his hands and twiddled his thumbs. The scarred table top appeared to fascinate him.

Harvey prompted him. "What happened after you joined them in the kitchen?"

"R.J. had Gloria cornered against the wall, pinned there with an arm on either side." Mackenzie pushed his mug away. "He told her he'd heard about her birthday, and she wasn't jail bait anymore.

"Gloria's eyes were wide, and she pushed with both hands against his chest. Amara pulled on his arm, trying to help Gloria. The girls stared at each other, neither one looked at Curwood. They were panicked. I could see it on their faces."

Mackenzie coughed out a short laugh. "But it was like they had some weird connection. Like combined power would win for them." His laugh trickled off in a full coughing fit. "But then I'd been reading Superman comics. And I was drunk. I don't think any of them saw me. I went toward them to get Curwood to lay off, but things got confused."

Mackenzie shook his head like a dog shedding water. "Gloria said she'd never sleep with him, she didn't like him, and she didn't like boys. She spit out the word 'boys.' R.J.'s jaw tensed and his eyes narrowed. I knew what was coming and I backed off. I'd seen his nasty look before. He'd drunk far too much, and his temper had boiled over."

Tempers fueled accidents that turned into murders. "Did he always have a temper?"

"Oh yes, anyone close to him knew about it. He did a damn good job of keeping it in check, but when it burst out, man, you didn't want to be anywhere near him."

Harvey glanced over and read Nat's note. *Find witnesses to R.J.'s temper.* Another nail to shape for his coffin.

He shifted his attention back to Mackenzie. Sweat dotted the man's forehead, and his body slumped as if in defeat. "When his temper was uncontrolled, did he ever hurt anyone?"

Mackenzie shifted his eyes, looked down the kitchen and back.

Now that's suggestive. Harvey cleared his throat and Mackenzie's attention snapped back to the conversation.

"Maybe. One time at a beach party." He stopped.

Obviously, Mackenzie still had a reluctance to sharing what he knew. Were they going to have to pull details out of him, one at a time? Harvey prompted with the next obvious question. "What about the time at the beach party?"

"One night a hippie gave him a hard time. Called him up-tight and boring. Said no wonder he couldn't get laid." Mackenzie licked his lips and ran one hand down over them. He looked around and lowered his voice, as if the wrong person would hear him. "R.J. beat the crap out of the guy before we could pull him off."

Now that's significant. But we need other witnesses to corroborate. Harvey glanced at Nat. She caught his tag and jumped in. "Can you tell us who else saw this?"

Mackenzie looked up, way up, avoiding their joint attention. "Not sure. Another drunk-up night. Not good for remembering stuff. And I'd never met most of them before or since."

Harvey resumed interview control. "We'll come back to the beating." Most important was getting the full murder story. Backup could come later. "Before we go on with what happened on August sixteenth, would you like more coffee or water?"

"What I'd like is another beer." The man licked his lips again. "There's some in the fridge."

Harvey noted his reason for turning off the recorder and pushed back his chair. In the fridge he bypassed the beer and found two cans of cola. He brought one and handed it to Mackenzie. "There you go." He restarted the recorder. "Resuming the interview," he said. "Did you know why the girls were there?"

Mackenzie drank half the cola at one go and hiccupped. "They didn't say. But I'd heard at the store they'd taken off, like runaways you know. I guess they were hiding out."

"On the night in question, August 15 to 16, 1969, did Curwood keep his temper in control?"

Mackenzie blustered. "He started taunting Gloria. Like, *I'd bet you'd like a man. Why don't you let me show you how good it can be?* And other stuff. And Amara yelled at him and said didn't he get it. She and Gloria were a couple and they did NOT like men or boys like him."

Harvey maintained his gaze on the man's face and concentrated on both the words and his own shock.

"Oh boy, he went off like a rocket. He shook off Amara and pushed her. Man, he could look ugly when he let fly. He shouted, said they both needed a damn good... well, you know. And he'd give it to them, and they'd change their minds." Mackenzie's hands underscored his words. "He grabbed Gloria's hair and pressed his body against her. Once he had her trapped, he grabbed her jaw so she couldn't turn her head and kissed her."

He paused, shuddered. "Brutal. Amara climbed on his back and beat on his head. Man, all hell broke loose. I'm not sure how things happened. Everything got tangled up and both girls went flying." Mackenzie swept a hand out.

Beside Harvey, Nat tensed and put an arm on his arm. They sat for a moment. The storyteller of and the listeners to a horrific tale.

"Amara fell to the floor. Gloria went down, hit her head on the stove and landed on her back." He gulped, his sentence chopped short and shooting out of him. "Amara screamed and crawled to Gloria. R.J. backed off with his hands grabbing the back of his head and an 'oh shit' look on his face." Mackenzie buried his face in his hand, his shoulders shaking.

Holy crap. That's more than I expected. It's a tale out of a bloody B-Movie.

Mackenzie's sobs peppered the silence. Harvey turned to Nat. Her eyes wide, her mouth open she stared back. *As shocked as I am.* He blew out, ran a hand over his head and looked back at Mackenzie.

We're not talking about any old killer, we're talking about a respected police officer. What chaos will come from this?

"Taking a break," he said, added the time and turned off the recorder. He needed to process the information and the ramifications.

Nat pushed to her feet. "Coffee," she said and headed for the coffee machine. She started a fresh pot and stood, staring out the window. No doubt processing her own reactions. *Her brain must be racing as fast as mine.*

Harvey got the second cola from the fridge, popped it open and set it front of Mackenzie.

Backing away, Harvey leaned against the counter beside Nat, arms folded and eyes closed. *How in hell are we going to deal with this?*

****

Ten minutes later, Nat handed Harvey the coffee. She stood shoulder-to-shoulder with him while they both took their first sips. "Ready?" she asked.

Harvey nodded. "I'm ready. You?"

"Guess so." She led the way back to the table.

Turning on the recording, Harvey read in the time and those present. The steadiness in his voice surprised him. His innards were quivering like jelly in a high storm.

Matt Mackenzie, sober now, but with his hands shaking, resumed his story. "Gloria had her scalp split. And the blood? My God, the blood. I knew nothing about first aid. I grabbed an old cushion and put it under her head. But her eyes stared, blank-like. One last breath came out of her. It wasn't loud or raspy or anything, but I'll never forget it." Mackenzie laid both palms flat on the table and stared at them.

As if he'd forgotten the interview, he sat there for long minutes, flicking his right forefinger against his thumb. Finally, he breathed in and jump-started his story.

"Man, Amara screeched like a banshee and flew at Curwood, yelling and swearing and scratching, beating on his face. I tried to stop her," he muttered. "I really did try."

He went on in a rough voice. "But she kicked back and caught my kneecap, and I went down. When I got up, R.J.'s hands were around her neck." Mackenzie demonstrated, wrapping his hands around air. "He seemed to be pushing her, or shaking her, to make her shut up.

"And then her face got red, her breath gurgled and she clawed at his hands. And, then her eyes rolled." Mackenzie dropped his head back and let his eyes roll up. "And she hung there looking like my sister's rag doll."

Talk about things gone wrong. But all that clawing, maybe left blood under her fingernails—if we can find her body. In his peripheral vision, Harvey saw Nat make her own notes.

"R.J. snapped out of it, jerked away and let her fall. I checked for a pulse. Not there." Mackenzie's head wagged, his countenance flat. His voice whispered the next words. "I swore at him. Told him he'd damn well killed them both." He stopped and worried one hand against the other as he inspected the side wall.

Harvey spoke into the void. "Let me clarify." He cleared his throat. "Both girls—on the floor, dead. One with a head injury and the other strangled. Is that correct?"

Mackenzie nodded without looking up.

"Please confirm orally for the recording."

"Yes, that is correct." Mackenzie rubbed his hands over his head and clasped them behind his neck. "Boy, I sobered up fast. I ran to the sink and puked. Behind me, I could hear R.J. pacing up and down and muttering. I wiped my mouth and went back. I suggested I go and find the nearest phone and call for help."

But the police were never called. Natalie asked the question. "How did he react?"

"He told me not to be stupid. If we told anyone, we'd both end up in jail."

Mackenzie repeated his head-rubbing action. "I said it was an accident. He said, even if we could prove it was accidental, it would take months, maybe longer and our careers would be ruined." Mackenzie snorted. "What he meant was his career would be ruined. I didn't have one."

The recitation seemed far-fetched. If they hadn't found Gloria's body, and blood in the kitchen, Harvey would not have believed Mackenzie's story. "What did you do?"

"You know what we did. I listened to him and helped him dig holes to bury them. We found some little bushes in the woods and transplanted them over the graves to cover the digging. I guess one was a tree. The storm covered everything and pounded the dirt on the grave-sites flat."

He rhymed off the information, his monotone words coming out in puffs. "We found a bucket and lugged water from the old well.

"We washed everything, sluiced water over the floor.

"We took an old coat hanging in the back entry and sopped up the water.

".R.J. took care of any fingerprints he could think of. At least he said he did. We buried the coat too, in a different spot."

Harvey glanced at Nat. *Another item to dig up.* The extra beeps from the metal detector might have been coat buttons. Finding them would confirm Mackenzie's story. And if they were really lucky, there would be residual blood on the buttons.

Tears ran down Mackenzie's face. He rubbed his cheeks with his fists. "By then it was mid-morning and the sea was much calmer. We headed back and said we got caught by the storm." He purged his lungs of air. "Mr. Harris said we did the right thing, waiting. But he charged us extra anyway. For once, R.J. didn't object. His dad showed up after lunch and took us back to the other island and to the mainland and we were back in Halifax by Sunday night." He shrugged and stopped.

Harvey frowned. "Did you ever mention it again? Especially when the body washed up and was identified as Gloria Roberts?" he asked.

Mackenzie shook his head. "R.J. came to see me. Said he'd kill me, too. Or fix evidence that he wasn't even there and put all the blame on me. He said he'd wiped off his own fingerprints but had made sure to leave mine in the room. I believed him. Scheming bastard."

And back then, DNA testing wasn't available. All the blood in the province wouldn't have helped prove who killed the girls.

Mackenzie crushed the empty pop can between his hands. "Me, I have trouble living with it. I suffered from nightmares and took to drinking." He looked around his shabby kitchen. "You can see where I ended up."

Mackenzie was done. Harvey noted the time and people present and turned off the recorder. He looked at Nat. "Quite a tale," he said.

"But you'll be able to keep me safe, right?" Mackenzie's voice rose a notch.

Harvey nodded. "We'll do our damnedest. Let's chat," he said to Nat and nodded toward the living room.

Standing by the window, they both crossed their arms and stood silent. Mackenzie's sobs stopped. Harvey turned and faced Nat.

"Like my dad said," she said. "Everyone talks sooner or later. This information is damning, but our work isn't done."

Harvey snorted. "No kidding. We need a watertight case. Statements, forensics including DNA, and witnesses." He glanced behind. "That means this one, too. Patsy will testify. The paper documents will help."

Outside, dusk shrouded the landscape in black and gray layers. "Meanwhile, we need to put him somewhere," Harvey said, jerking his head toward the kitchen. "And not in any place known to the police. This is one time we have to protect a witness against our own."

"It feels counterintuitive," she said. "But you're right. Any suggestions."

Turner? Eddie, the rookie? No, we can't involve them and risk their reputations. Information is one thing. Hiding a witness quite another. "What about Lem and Jackson? They have military backgrounds and they know the coast and area." *And they'll be happy to cooperate.*

"Works for me," Nat said. "You call Jackson, and I'll get in touch with Lem."

Harvey ran a hand down her arm and grasped her fingers. "This is going to be brutal," he said, "are you ready for it?"

She nodded. "Bring it on. We have both law and justice on our side. I can take media frenzies and slurs against me. I can't let a murderer go unpunished."

"You're one strong lady," Harvey said and kissed her hand. "And remember--"

She smiled. "I know, you've got my back."

Thirty minutes later, Harvey escorted Mackenzie out the back door and through the shadows to the car. He tucked him in on the back floor and hid him under a plaid blanket. Going to the driver's door, he called toward the house. "I'll see you in the morning."

Nat stood in the doorway and raised a hand to acknowledge his farewell. He knew her next moves. She'd step out, turn back and instruct the non-existent person inside to lock the door behind her. *Misdirection never hurts.*

And I have a lot to accomplish before dawn. Passing Mackenzie over to Jackson, meeting with Turner, and making detailed lists and notes would take time. Turner had turned down the option of pulling out of their investigation. Now they needed to compile evidence and to back up Mackenzie's story. He rolled through Chester and onto the secondary highway. *And luck by the barrel full wouldn't hurt either.*

****

Full dark covered the landscape by the time Natalie reached the cabin. She entered her code on the secured gate and gained access. As exhausted as she was, she wasn't finished for the night. She had records to photograph, emails to send, notes to compile and a timeline to nail down. And an extra step—Devon was a commissioner of oaths. Certified photocopies wouldn't be remiss as backup either.

She locked the cabin's front door behind her. *And in the morning we have to fold Harvey's lists into mine. And then who do we give the information to? The CSIS branch of the Mounties? The Nova Scotia Police Complaints Commission? The Police Review Board?* More than a complaint of harassment or minor misconduct charge, accusing an officer of murder loomed gigantically.

Brayburn. Dump it in his lap and let him decide which agency got the evidence. What call would he make? She'd like to believe it would be the right one.

She placed her call to Devon. "Hey, I have documents I need copied and certified. Can we meet in the office later?"

"Tonight?"

"Yes. It's critical. I'll call you when I'm ready."

"Okay. But I'm making a pizza. I can't work late at night on an empty stomach."

Natalie laughed and went into the kitchen to put on the kettle.

Taking out the appropriate ledger, she started with the front page and worked through to the end. Context gave all the critical points meaning. She set her watch down beside the page listing Mackenzie's boat-rental. The extra time and date would confirm when she took the shot. Compiling all photos, she sent an email to her private computer in the city and to Greg's business email. A third copy went to Harvey who would print it all.

Opting for hot chocolate, she settled with her notebook and, point by point, wrote out Mackenzie's story. On another page, she outlined the information from Patsy Creaser regarding Curwood's presence at the final identification of the body in the graveyard. Harvey would have the signed and witnessed affidavit from Patsy regarding her statement. And Lem would write out his statement, sign it and get it witnessed for the morning.

She transferred the metal detector results to email and forwarded them. She wrote up the procedure and results and the events of Bob the dog's visit. Turner would need to sign a statement about Bob's work. She called Harvey and asked him to get it and Lem's statements. *And I need statements from Lenya and Mrs. Gerber as well. Better to have the full picture than to miss one tiny point.*

Finally, she put down the pen and stretched. The clock showed that two hours had passed. She called Devon and stacked the evidence to take for safekeeping. Mr. Harris's extra, unneeded documents she returned to the bankers' boxes to go back to the museum. Finally, leaving one light on, she set out across the dark yard toward the main building.

"Hey," Devon said, meeting Natalie at the office door. "What's up?" She wagged a finger. "Is there a report I haven't received yet?"

"Oh yes, I have things to tell you," Natalie said. She pushed her hair back from her forehead, weariness screaming through her body. "I'll start photocopying while you read. It's spellbinding."

The two set to work, pizza at hand to boost their energy. Devon exclaimed often as she came to critical points. Finally, the copies were made and certified. All pertinent pictures were printed and digital copies sent to join the other emailed documents.

"This is hard to take in," Devon said. "If I hadn't seen all this with my own eyes, I would have doubted it for sure. And you have Mackenzie's story all on tape as well?"

"Sure as I'm settin' here," Natalie said. "Harvey will be making copies and locking up the original." She looked across the room. "What time is it? I'm exhausted."

"Close to midnight," Devon said. "Let's put this stuff in the safe and you can head to bed."

"No argument from me. We'll lock the copies in the desk." She leaned forward and pulled to her feet. "Enough is enough." The final steps took only ten minutes and Natalie headed to the cabin. Outside, a steady rain fell, soaking the landscape. A blurred moon attempted to breach the clouds with only minimal success. Muscles and bones protested her long day. *I should sleep like a rock.*

In her temporary living room, she stretched, rolled her head and looked right and left to loosen the kinks in her neck. Prickles crawled up her spine. She glanced around. *There's nobody here unless Harvey is already back.* But his car wasn't there, and his bedroom door stood open. *Besides, he'd have joined us in the office or waited up for me. I'm tired and imagining things.*

She turned off the lamp she'd left on earlier and stood in the dim light until she could see. With minimal lighting outside, darkness settled around her. She edged her way to the bedroom, washed her face and gave her teeth a cursory brushing. Shedding her clothing, she pulled on her favorite long jersey and some bottoms.

The bed felt wonderful, and she stretched out with a yawn. *Where's my phone?* The thought jerked her back from sleep. Groggily, she made it to the living room and back with the phone in hand. About to put it on the bedside table, a better-safe-than-sorry-moment struck her and she slid it under her pillow instead.

CHAPTER SIXTEEN

Later, Natalie wasn't sure what woke her. Immobilized, she maintained even breathing. The floor creaked. *That's the spot two steps outside the bedroom.* I have company. *And it's not Harvey. He'd avoid the squeaky bit.*

Fabric rustled, removing the option to return to sleep. She opened her eyes a slit and let the gray and grayer in the room register. A darker shadow appeared beside the bed. Her best guess in the dim light put it at six foot plus dressed in black. Dark against dark.

She took in a slow, sleep-like breath. *Aftershave? I know the scent. Curwood.* The only man in the area taller than Turner, and one who wore that aftershave. She flexed her fingers under the pillow and found the phone, pushing the record button by feel. *Oh crap, what does he know? And how did he find out?*

She closed her eyes too late. He'd seen them open. "Don't be coy, Parker. You know I'm here." His hand pressed her head against the pillow, and something pricked her neck, stinging and burning.

"Curwood. What the hell are you doing?"

Lassitude inched through her limb after limb. *I can't pass out. Not safe.* She tried to scream but her voice croaked and her words slurred. *There's no one to hear me.* She managed a partial question. "What - you - inject?" *Will it kill me?*

Curwood pulled the blankets off her. "Don't worry, you won't pass out right away. You couldn't let it go, could you? I convinced Brayburn to relegate it to the cold cases and to suspend you. All I needed was six months."

He bent over her and slid one arm under her shoulders. "Come on, Parker. Sit up for me."

"Why?"

"You don't think I'd let this get any further, do you? I have too much at stake." He pulled her into a sitting position. "I'm not giving up a good retirement and an award because of those stupid girls." He shifted his stance and pulled her feet off the bed.

"Not my fault it happened. They should NOT have fought me. Besides, the deaths were accidents."

Is he talking to me or himself?

He managed to get her seated on the side of the bed. "Not my fault the silly girl fell against the stove." He grabbed Natalie under her armpits and lifted. "Come on, up on your feet. Now walk." Alternately dragging and supporting, he led her toward the main room.

And what about the second girl? No accident there. Her brain worked but her mouth didn't.

She slumped, unable to control her limbs. *Maybe gravity will pull me into an uncooperative lump on the floor.* It didn't happen. For an old guy, Curwood had impressive strength. At the patio door, she stumbled and lurched onto the deck. Gravity won and down she went, a slithering, misshapen heap.

Curwood muttered obscenities. He stretched her flat and dragged her into a fireman's carry. He staggered once, got his balance and started up the hill.

What's he going to do? Bury me? She almost giggled. Up there wasn't a smart place to put a new body. *Body. I do not want to be a body.*

He paused behind the old house and looked over the yard. "I saw the markers. They're gone now and the ground tamped down. No one will take the word of a kid with a metal detector."

He doesn't know about Turner and Bob the dog.

Her middle pressed painfully against his shoulder, her head bobbed on his back, and her hands dangled uselessly below his belt. *The man has no butt.*

Inside, he lowered her to the floor and shifted to dragging her by both armpits. Her heels thumped up the stairs, step by step.

Hopscotch. Up the stairs.

He gave one last tug and rolled her into the empty bedroom, the one on the right.

She commanded her limbs to move but her muscles refused to listen to her brain. Tossed on her side, she could only listen and stare ahead. *Look, he has the bankers' boxes from the museum. So sad, too bad, Devon has the good stuff.*

"Relax," he said and laughed harshly. "You'll be out cold soon. A mixed medication dose allowed me to move you, but its full effect will hit soon." He knelt, rolled her on her back and fold her arms over her chest.

Natalie tried to move again. Her eyes shifted slightly, and one finger twitched. *Come on body. Fight it.*

Curwood pulled a panel off the wall.

There's long storage space under the eaves. But what does he want to store?

In moments she found out. He grabbed her under the armpits and hauled her to the opening. He slid her feet in first and pushed her shoulders until he had her body stuffed in. He took a last look at her. "You are too damn smart for your own good." He poked her with a stick. "But you won't get out. With this wedged against the panel, it won't move, even if you do."

He withdrew. A moment later she heard a rough scratch and smelled the pungent odor of a struck match. *Oh God, no. Not fire.* Her protest only made a groan, and he laughed.

"Don't worry. If you're lucky, you'll either be out cold by the time the flames get to you or the smoke will have done you in. Those ledgers make a good fire starter, and with a little help, it'll consume this whole place. When they find you, they'll figure you got too close to the killer. No one saw me leave Halifax. No one saw me arrive here. And no one can see us now. Never be a suspect."

Oops, the ship has sailed on that one. You ARE a suspect.

"Mackenzie won't be around for long." He laughed. "And I'll be back home in bed by the time they call to tell me the bad news."

The moonlight disappeared and scraping sounds marked the stick being wedged against the panel. Wisps of smoke snuck under it. Adrenalin surged through her, bile burned her throat and a pounding pulse covered all further sound. *I'm going to die. She couldn't move, couldn't think and couldn't even scream.* The drug reached maximum effect and rendered her unconscious.

****

Smoke. Hot shivers raced over her skin.

Roaring flames. Her middle puddles with ice.

Coming for me. Her muscles, still partially immobilized, jerked spasmodically.

No, no, no. She faded in and out of puddles of awareness and wells of terror.

Barking. A dog. Mutt?

She hunched her shoulder and pulled up her knees. In her mind, she could see herself do it. But only one hand and a foot had moved. *I'm going to die.* The thought ripped through again and she sobbed.

The barking penetrated her hearing a second time. *No. I can't be afraid. Mutt. Keep barking, boy.* Her arms jerked and she managed to control one hand.

She laughed through her tears. *I'm moving. Yes, be strong.*

Pinching her lips together, she closed her eyes and summoned a memory of Mutt running on the beach.

There's soft wind, mist. The gulls are screeching. I'm okay. But there's danger. I have to call him back. She kept her eyes closed.

"Can I yell?" She muttered, talking to only herself. She yelled. "Mutt, get help." Hoarse words barely reached her ears, never mind Mutt's. But the words were more defined than earlier. She shortened her call. *Help.*

Again and again, she cleared her throat, drew in smoke-tinged air and pushed the word out. Frantic barking continued outside. Sure the dog was sounding an alarm, she turned her attention to her next step.

Need to move. Adrenalin counteracts drugs. The explosion, harness your fear from it, be afraid for just a moment. And use that fear.

Adrenalin surged through her. She inched her fingers up the wall, fighting the lethargy in her arm. Creeping her hand sideways, she hit a joist. *The attic space. I'm in the attic space.*

Curwood put me here. Drugged me. Move, damn it. She curled her fingers again, used them to creep her arm forward. She pulled, got her body into a face-down position. Her head turned to one side and rough wood dug into her cheek. Commanding one limb at a time, she made it to all fours and knelt there, swaying.

Where is the hatch? She shifted, her shoulder connected with the sloped wall. Her fingers edged into the seam between hatch-door and wall. A push confirmed he'd braced it. The effort tipped her and once again she lay on her side. Closer to the hatch, but back on her side.

Think. Visualize the panel from the outside. Where would he brace the stick? Against the center. *And the hatch goes out.* She hitched around until her feet were against the panel. Rocking like a baby learning to roll over, she made it onto her back, edged her feet up one side of the panel and pushed. With pressure on one side only, the panel tilted and a lighter darkness became visible. A two-footed kick, as weak as it was, dislodged the panel. She worked her toes into the gap and pushed sideways. The panel fell free. No longer restrained, a whoosh of mixed air and smoke swirled into the space.

Inhaling, she coughed body-shaking coughs. *Come on. Move.* She pulled the jersey over her mouth as best she could and laboriously got on her belly and commando crawled out the opening. Smoke formed in layers above the floor and swirled and pooled along the ceiling line.

Scrabbling, she moved perpendicular to the wall, and still using the commando crawl, inched across the room, over rotting and torn linoleum until she touched the far wall. Looking up she saw the grayness showing between the slats of the boarded-up window. She'd made it.

The smoke thickened, and she looked behind her. The flames on the landing licked at the door frame and took bites out of the flooring. *The window is my only way out.* But the effort sapped her energy, and she slouched against the wall beneath the window.

Outside, Mutt barked frantically. It was the last sound she heard.

****

Harvey crossed the beach road toward the bridge to the island.

No street lights out there to illuminate his way, and the car's headlamps cut a slice through the darkness. The moon escaped the cloud cover for brief moments, exposing the bridge and ramp. On the far side, he started up the slope to the main road. A car cut him off and he jammed on his brakes, yanked the wheel and barely missed it. The other car revved its motor and rolled on, thumping onto the bridge and clattering into the night.

What the heck? No lights. Not a glimmer. He stepped out and peered after the vehicle. *And no running lights.* He ducked back into his seat and fastened the safety belt. Closing his eyes, he solidified his memory. *A newer model car. It should have had running lights.* Uneasiness cloaked his shoulders.

Why were they running dark? He popped his car into gear and spewed loose gravel as he accelerated onto the road. *And who is out and about and in a hurry this time of night?*

The gate at the estate swung open without his code. Adrenalin surged through him. His internal trouble meter blared in his ears. Parking by Nat's vehicle, he raced toward Cabin Three.

Inside, dark shadows obscured his vision. In the kitchen, he turned on the bulbs over the stove. Faint light filtered into the living room. *She's not there.* He shook his head, rising above his panic. By this time she'd be well asleep in her room. Wouldn't she?

He crept across the room, avoiding the squeaky board. Her door stood open an inch. He gripped the edge and pushed. In the shadows beyond, he registered an empty bed and tossed bedding. *What the heck? Where's Nat? Bathroom?*

The bathroom door stood open and darkness gaped beyond. The uneasiness grabbed tighter.

"Nat. Natalie. Are you there?" No answer.

He flipped on the light, blinked at the brightness. *Slippers by the bed. Housecoat on the chair.* A dark corner under the pillow caught his eye. He lifted the cushion and found her cell phone. Its green light glowed. On and recording. Why did she leave it here? *Not a good sign.* Dread driving him, he accessed the recording.

"Curwood, what the hell are you doing?" Nat's voice, muffled but understandable. Panic slapped him hard. He listened intently until he heard Curwood order her to stand. He hit the off button and shoved the phone into his pocket. Frantic energy pushed him out the door. He ran to the patio and found the sliding door ajar.

He rammed it fully open. Stepped out on the deck. Stopped to listen, hoping for some sound in the night air. *Barking up the hill.*

His flying leap off the deck carried him a good four feet. He raced up the hill. Halfway up, the breath he sucked in came with smoke. Smoke, with flames skirting the lazy column, rose skyward. He pulled out his phone and dialed Devon's number. "Fire in the old house. Nat's there. Get help."

And his attention narrowed to a spearhead focus. He raced toward the old house with one thought in his mind. *Dear God, let me get to her in time.*

****

Natalie coughed, the rasp in her ears and the smothering sensation, pulling her to consciousness. *Hot, it's too hot.* She rolled, and her head connected with a hard surface. The one hand seemed to work, and she reached up. She'd hit a wall. *The wall in the old house.* A shriek ripped from her, ending in more coughing. *Fire. He left me to burn.*

Barking penetrated the fog in her head. *Barking? Right, I heard Mutt.*

"Nat. Nat." An urgent voice rose over the barking.

Only Harvey calls me Nat.

Mutt barked faster, louder.

He's outside. The veranda is outside this room. I need to yell.

She rolled, reached up and managed to grasp the window sill. She made it to her knees and peered out between the bottom slat and the sill. Wind gusted and flames roared and blazed off to her right.

She braced, pulled her shirt over her mouth and drew in as much fresh air as she could. "Here, over the veranda." The shout left her coughing but she managed and made another cry for help.

"I hear you. I'm coming."

Laughter and tears flooded Natalie. *Coming for me.* She looked back at the room. Flames licked along the wall beside her. Blue and green. Snapping and snarling. *Coming for me.*

Who will win? She crouched and put her head close to the floor. Slightly cooler air eased the ache in her lungs and dryness in her throat. A half dozen breaths and she tried again, reaching and pulling up. Her fingers closed over the window's handle and she pushed. The window refused to move. *Stuck. Or locked.*

No way could she pull herself up high enough to check the lock. *Break the window.* Smoke drifted down, pushed by the heavier layer above her. She brought her nose close to the floor, coughing.

Old single pane windows. Should break. But how? No shoes. No furniture. If she used her hands, she could cut herself badly.

Wrap your arm.

With what?

Options?

P.J. trousers.

Trousers it is.

She managed to get them off, stuck her arm top-down into one leg. Pulled it up and pushed inside the other. Wrapping any extra fabric around her hand, she made one more foray into the smoke swirling around her head and staining the glass gray.

Two good punches did the job, and the glass shattered. Fresh air swooshed in, washing over her face and, as she sucked it in, cooling her lungs. The air rushed past her and the fire ate it up, rising higher and faster. She collapsed on the floor again, tears from smoke and relief running down her face. *There are still the boards over the window.*

"Nat, Nat, can you hear me?"

Harvey. "Yes."

Dried wood released a nail and a squeal rent the air. *The wood is going. I can get out.*

"Can you push against the bottom board?"

"Yes." She struggled up and pushed.

Harvey pulled. Another nail protested and gave with the combined effort.

They tackled the next board and cleared the lower half of the window.

Fabric appeared and draped over the bottom, covering any glass bits left behind.

"Come on. Let's get you out of there." And there he was, backlit by moonlight and reaching for her. He extended his hands through the window.

She grabbed them and pulled up, wracked by coughs. Steadied by Harvey, she put one leg out the opening. He guided her leg until she felt the veranda roof under her foot. She ducked her head and tucked her upper body out after it.

"Pull," she said, "I can't get leverage."

Harvey shifted, wrapped his arms around her torso and lifted her out.

She collapsed on the roof, Harvey's solid bulk behind her. Matt barked frantically from below.

"Hurry."

Devon's voice. Where did she come from?

"Come on," Harvey said and scooted his butt toward the edge overhanging the lawn. "I'll lower you as far as I can, but you'll have to drop from there."

"What about you? How did you get up?"

"Shimmied up the support at the end. Don't worry, I'll hang off the edge and drop. It'll work."

Flames licked from the main building and up from below. They shot out the window, heating the air over Natalie's head. The remaining asphalt shingles seared her bare feet and knees. Her top inched up and pain registered on her bare bottom. She stretched flat and rolled to the edge.

High piercing blasts sliced the night. She jerked, startled by the siren from the old church.

Harvey steadied her and wrapped his hands around her wrists. "Grab my wrists." The grip established, she slid over the lip of the roof. Harvey lowered her until she dangled above the ground, as close as he could get her.

"On three," he said, "let go."

He counted and she fell. Landing on her feet, her balance failed and she fell backward. Above her, Harvey slid over the edge. He dropped and landed beside her, falling onto his back, too.

He turned his head and grinned at her. "We make one hell of a team."

Crying and laughing, she agreed. She rolled toward him and found herself wrapped in his arms. Solid, secure and.... "You had my back," she whispered against his face.

He answered with a kiss and deepened it until a different fire seared her body.

Mutt intruded, licking her neck and wiggling his body. He got between them and licked Harvey's face. Harvey sat, wrapped his arms around the dog and pulled him down in a partial wrestle.

Devon knelt beside Nat. "Are you two okay?"

Wracked by a coughing fit, Natalie croaked but got out her answer. "Couldn't be better." She ruffled Mutt's ears. "Good dog." Another coughing fit interrupted. "You'll get a steak every day this week."

Crashing announced the fire engine making progress on the newly cut road. Vie and Frank burst from the bushes and raced around the house to join Devon. Willing hands helped Nat and Harvey up and supported them as they ran from the burning building.

"We called the fire department," Devon said, somewhat unnecessarily. "The other engines will come down from the mainland and control the fire from spreading through the bush. But it's a good thing it rained overnight."

The smoky, scruffy bunch stood inside the ridge of bush and trees watching the flames. Natalie, snuggled in Harvey's arms, let tears run down her face. *So close. So like the explosion.* She turned her head and kissed Harvey's chin. *A third time might be my end. I need to make some changes.*

****

Harvey stood with both arms wrapped around Nat. Her shivers vibrated against him and smoke odor teased his nose. Tear tracks traced down her sooty face. Her scorched shirt reeked of smoke. Her bare legs must be cold, and her bare feet were undoubtedly cut and bruised. She needed care. *But I need to stay here.*

"Vie?" He caught the older woman's attention. "Can you and Devon take Nat down and take care of her? She's been hit with more than one over-the-top shock tonight."

Vie nodded and she and Devon got on either side of Nat. "Come on, honey. Let's get you cleaned up and get some hot, sugared tea into you."

Nat managed a laugh. "Tea," she said, "the cure-all of Caleb's Cove." She shifted her weight from Harvey's side and allowed Vie and Devon to support her. "Aren't you coming?" she asked Harvey.

"I'll be along soon," he said, "but I can help here. Go on. Vie will take care of you." He kissed her forehead and watched her go. *Strong lady. She'll survive. The two of us are solid. But will our careers survive the accusations against Curwood?*

He reached for his toothpick and found only bare skin. His shirt still covered the broken glass up at the window. Naked from the waist up, he headed for the line holding a water hose.

We need a plan, a good one, and we need to get to Brayburn for help as soon as possible. A plan formed as he assisted with the snaking hose.

More men streamed onto the site, each carrying whatever gear and equipment they could. When the water truck emptied, they resorted to fire extinguishers, axes, shovels and fire-beating canvasses. The water truck soaked the house before running out.

The crew focused their efforts on containing the house fire and preventing leaps of flames starting other fires in the woods. Hot, dangerous work but there were no complaints. The soaked ground and undergrowth made the job easier. They dug trenches, felled dead trees and put out spot fires.

Fresh volunteers relieved Harvey and he retreated to the edge of the action. *Thank goodness, we can always rely on the residents of the Cove no matter what the problem.*

Finally, the trucks from the mainland arrived and their sirens wailed one last time. Their water truck pulled up the old driveway as far as it could and soon hoses sprayed the house fire. Burning fast and furious, it had managed to consume the dry wood.

With a crash and roar, the roof and walls caved. Water made its mark until the fallen, charred timber glowed and smoked. The danger past, two of the men left the crew and headed for Harvey. Doucette, the fire chief from the main land and Jackson Ritcey, the local volunteer organizer, came looking for information. They pulled off their helmets and gloves as they came.

The mainland chief took the lead. "Devon Ritcey called in the blaze, but I understand you found it. Tell me what you know."

"I got back late from the mainland, arrived minutes before sunrise actually, and I heard the dog barking." He pointed at Mutt lolling by his feet, "He'd found bones up here before so I thought I'd see what had excited him this time. Halfway up the hill, I smelled smoke, called Devon and came up. The blaze engulfed the main floor and flames were visible in the upstairs windows." A vague plan started in his head and he left out Natalie's rescue. "You know the rest."

"Did you see anyone? Kids, someone who might have accidentally, or intentionally, set the fire?"

"Ah," Harvey said. "At the bridge, a car running without lights almost ran me off the road. I didn't get a good look. Late model, dark color, male driver. Don't know if he was coming from here but he certainly was in a hurry."

"Thanks, not much to go on. Inspectors will check the wreckage once it's cold." Doucette shook hands and returned to his crew.

Jackson remained. He waited until the fire chief was out of hearing and asked his question. "So, what's the rest of the story?"

"Nat was in the house," Harvey said, his voice harsh. "I barely got her out in time."

Jackson's shocked curse echoed in Harvey's head. He dropped his chin to his chest and stared at the ground, his jaw working. *I want to find the bastard and beat the crap out of him.*

"Who did it?" Jackson asked. "And how do we get him?"

"We'll get him." *But I need to do it right.* "But finish up here and come down to the house. I'll need your help." He turned and stomped through the bush toward the lawn. *Curwood will pay for this big time.*

CHAPTER SEVENTEEN

Back at the cabin, Natalie lay tucked up on the sofa, her hands and feet bandaged, her throat benefiting from a warm, soothing drink. She'd stood in the shower until the water ran cold. Fresh clothing helped, but the smell lingered in her nostrils. *Maybe a neti pot would help.*

Vie tended to Natalie's wounds and served the ginger-peach tea. She settled Natalie on the sofa and tucked a quilt around her. "You sleep, child. Lord knows you need it." Vie kissed her on top of the head and left.

Natalie dozed. *I'll rest till Harvey comes, then we need to get busy.*

The patio door slid open and Harvey stepped in. He observed her for long minutes. "You're a sight for sore eyes, girl." He knelt beside her and pulled her against him. His face buried against her neck, he inhaled. "And you smell so good."

She welcomed his warmth. "I'm not going to smell good for long. You smell smoky."

He pulled back. "Some thanks for rescuing the maiden from the fiery dragon."

"Hmm, I suppose I should consider you *helped* me escape." He leaned against the sofa and rested his head on her middle.

"Saucy wench. No gratitude."

Silence wrapped them tight. Natalie brushed soot from his hair and smoothed a hand over his cheek. Minutes ticked by. Finally, Harvey sat up and taking her face in his hands, kissed her, his lips soft. The sensation flooded her, and she returned the kiss.

They were both breathing hard by the time they broke apart. Harvey put his forehead against hers. "Don't you ever scare me again," he whispered.

A short time later they crossed the yard, hand in hand. Lights shone from the kitchen windows. Half of the Cove's inhabitants had joined Devon, Vie and Frank. Adam raced to them as soon as they entered. Natalie knelt and hugged him.

He whispered. "Are you okay?" She nodded. He stepped back. "Man, did you see that fire?" His mother joined him. "I'm glad you're okay," she said and pulled Adam away.

Others crowded around them with similar sentiments. Kelsey, Mrs. Gerber, Lily, Lenya as well as Jackson and Nancy, Wayne and Gwen, and Lem. A car pulled up outside and a knock on the door announced more people. Turner and the long-time rookie, Eddie, joined the melee.

"Nearly had a heart attack," Turner said, "when I heard the call come in." He shook Harvey's hand and offered Natalie a stiff hug.

Jackson and Turner dragged an armchair in from the sitting room for Natalie. Coffee, tea, eggs, and bacon went the rounds. Finally, Devon stepped up. "Enough chatter. If you're up to it, you two, can you please tell us the whole story?"

The chatter stopped and everyone settled to listen.

Harvey pulled over a high-backed stool and settled by Natalie, his hand possessively on the chair back. "You need to start," he said. "I missed the opening act."

"I got back to the cabin about twelve thirty," Natalie said. "After Devon and I secured the evidence." She folded her hands. "I barely managed to crawl into bed." She continued through the ordeal until the point where she heard Mutt barking as she passed out. Faces around the room reflected their horror.

"Meanwhile," Harvey said, "Jackson, Lem and I secured a crucial witness. It wasn't quite sunup when I got here. I found the cabin empty, Nat's bed thrown back but her slippers and robe still in place. I found her phone and a recording on it." He quoted what he'd heard and shock rippled around the room punctuated with gasps. He finished his story to the point where he stood looking up at the window over the veranda, the one Mutt had led him to.

Natalie finished up with her escape and Harvey's help. "And the firemen arrived and dealt with the fire." Everyone crowded around and Natalie accepted the offered hugs.

The men gathered in one corner and exchanged muttered

questions and threats.

All but Turner. "For a longtime police officer. Curwood hasn't been smart," he said, talking into Natalie's ear. "How on earth did he think destroying and killing you would keep him from being caught?"

"He thinks he has all evidence we've found and he's already adjusted the documents to support his version of the story." Natalie answered.

"And maybe he's counting on the old boy network to cover up the rest." Turner snorted. "I'll bet he spilled the coffee on the old report."

"I think you're correct," Natalie added. "All that, and more. Being backed into a corner brings out the worst in beast and man. That man displayed scary-cold anger, let me tell you."

Jackson asked the pressing question. "Do you have enough to arrest him?"

Harvey pulled out Nat's phone and hit the play button. Curwood's voice played into the room. He stopped the recording when Curwood ordered her to stand up.

Disbelief preceded muttered threats and shocked exclamations.

"And," Natalie added, "we have a written statement dictated and signed by the man who was with Curwood when he killed Gloria and Amara."

Off to the side, Mrs. Gerber gasped and brought her hand to her throat. Lenya hugged her, and Doris Roberts joined them.

"I'd hate to have been with Curwood when he didn't find the witness at home. Sounded to me he planned an adventure of the death kind for him too," Natalie said.

"But that witness," Jackson added, "is safely playing rum runner." Natalie looked at him, her brow furrowed.

"Emily's cave," Jackson said.

"Good place," she said. "Emily wasn't keen on it, but it certainly is secure." The cave, its entrance underwater at high tide, would keep Matt Mackenzie safe until they needed him. "You left him some blankets, food and a light, didn't you?"

Lem nodded. He raised a hand. "You said you were almost run off the road at the bridge?"

Harvey nodded.

"And can we assume it might have been Curwood?"

"Likely candidate," Harvey said. "Hard to know if he hung around to make sure the fire took or not. Or how fast it went to full blaze."

Lem glanced at Jackson. "What do you think?"

"Possible."

Natalie looked from one to the other. "What have you two been up to?"

Lem scratched his neck. "Remember the fire at the museum?"

As if they could forget. She'd missed it, but had seen the aftermath.

"Jackson and I decided to put in more outside lights after that." He paused.

Jackson continued. "We went a step further and put in security cameras."

Natalie jumped off her stool. "Any chance they reach to the road?" She faced Lem. "Tell me they do."

Lem gave a depreciating shrug. "As soon as we were asked to keep watch on the grave-sites, we adjusted the camera to record cars on the road."

Harvey grabbed the man and lifted him off the floor in a hug. "You sneaky old devil."

He set Lem down and turned to Natalie. "We'll get him, I know we will."

"What are you waiting for," Jackson said, "I'll go get the tape. You set up the machine in the office." He glanced at his watch. "What better time than seven a.m. to watch a movie?"

****

By mid-morning the same day they arrived in Halifax. Brayburn's calls to Natalie's phone had finally stopped. She'd chosen to stay off the grid. At the moment, she had her head adorned with one of Vie's colorful turbans, her eyes covered by dark glasses and her body decked in ordinary street clothes. She slouched in Turner's personal car, a well-restored Mustang.

Harvey and Eddie headed to the detachment office. They marched, shoulder-to-shoulder, into the building and upstairs to Brayburn's office. The man himself looked up when they crossed toward his corner office. He stood, glaring at them.

"Conrad. What the hell is going on? Why isn't Parker answering her phone? Curwood called in. His Intel from Caleb's Cove says she died in a fire. I don't believe it."

Curwood trying to cover his tracks, no doubt. The man hadn't wasted any time. Harvey nodded at Eddie who closed the office door and stood at ease blocking it. Eddie, he really should call him Ed, was there to provide witness to the chain of evidence and the upcoming report.

"Ah ha, eh? Curwood says he heard she's dead?" he said. "I wonder who told him." Two paces and he settled into the chair facing the desk. He pointed to Brayburn. "Sit down, sir. I have a lot to tell you."

Half an hour later, Brayburn paced the small area beside his desk. "I can't believe this. It's too fantastic! I mean, Curwood? He's a policeman's policeman. An icon in the department." He dropped back in his seat. "Proof," he demanded.

Harvey took his briefcase from Eddie. "These are certified copies." He pulled out the statement from Mackenzie and handed it over. The ledgers followed as well as Lem's statement. He pulled out the affidavits. "Here are the other backup documents outlining a timeline and Curwood's part in the wrongful identification of the body buried in Caleb's Cove graveyard."

Brayburn read. He unbuttoned his top shirt button, mopped his brow and worried his knuckles. Muttered exclamations and curses accompanied various points in the reading. Eventually, he looked up and sat back. "Unbelievable. All this is printed, how can we be sure it's not doctored? Or it's other people's narratives of the time. What will really prove it?"

Eddie handed Parker's phone to Harvey. They had a tape to leave with Brayburn, but wanted him to hear the original.

Harvey put it on the desk. "You'd recognize Curwood's voice, would you, sir?"

"Yes, certainly."

Harvey hit the go button, and Curwood's voice played in the room.

Brayburn turned a lighter shade of gray. "Turn that damn thing off."

After doing so, Harvey slid the last piece of evidence over to Brayburn. "This car almost ran me off the road shortly before I found the fire. You can see the make and model and a section of the plate. It tracks to Curwood's wife, but I'm sure last night's driver was male. The date and time stamp are there."

Brayburn tossed the picture on the pile and pushed the papers around. Eyes closed, he tipped back his head.

Harvey let him think.

Brayburn leaned forward and gathered the paper and pictures into a pile. "Leave these with me. I'll make the calls." He held up his hand as Harvey went to speak. "No, not to Curwood. I'll arrange meetings with two judges, and also representatives from CSIS, The Nova Scotia Police Complaints Commission, and The Police Review Board. I'll see the judges first and get a warrant for Curwood's arrest. I still have trouble wrapping my head around this," he said. "I've worked with this man for decades. He's been nothing but the poster child for the good and the just."

"That will be the popular opinion," Harvey said, "so we have to get this right and keep our evidence safe."

Brayburn nodded. "You still haven't told me about Parker. From your attitude, I assume she's not dead."

"She's alive and staying out of sight. All officers on the case agreed having a dead person turning up to confront Curwood would solidify the accusation."

"Really?" Brayburn's tone carried sarcasm. He sighed. "I suppose I owe her that much. Okay. You two head out. Stay hidden. This will take time. I'll try and get it in action for this evening. Strike while the iron is hot. Either way, I'll meet you at Curwood's house once I get a green light. He'll be willing to meet with me. Do you have a procedure in mind?"

Nice of him to ask. He could have bulldozed his way into taking over the whole arrest.

"We do," Harvey said and explained it all to Brayburn. "What do you think? Should we have members from more than one detachment on site for the final hoorah? Independent witnesses?"

"Works for me," Brayburn said. "Nothing I despise more than a crooked cop. And if he's crooked or not, we don't know, but murdering, or attempting to murder, a fellow officer is the absolute worst. And I use the term 'cop' in its worst connotation." He waved with one hand and picked up his phone in the other. "Now go on. I'll call you as soon as I can."

CHAPTER EIGHTEEN

The judges and official bodies moved uncharacteristically fast. By seven o'clock the same evening, various unmarked cars parked throughout Rey Curwood's neighborhood. Two men exited the car parked in the driveway at his Victorian house. The birds, settling in the early evening, provided marching music. Leafy trees filtered the early evening dimness to lace patterns on the ground.

Down the street, a man and woman exited an older model Mustang and strolled arm-in-arm through the posh neighborhood toward the same Victorian house. The woman's bright colored turban and jeans suggested she didn't live in the area. The tall, dark man by her side would draw uneasy looks if anyone looked out their window.

In the other direction, four uniformed officers waited under a huge oak, ready to move on the signal from Brayburn. Eddie, no longer called the rookie, commanded the search team and held the search warrant. Although out of his home jurisdiction, Eddie represented the Bridgewater detachment. A forensic team and a senior officer from CSIS slouched in their car a block away.

Conrad and Brayburn stepped in cadence to the raised front step. Harvey nodded at Brayburn and schooled his face in somber lines.

Brayburn adopted an appropriately concerned and sorrowful appearance. He patted his chest. "I'm wired and ready. Let's do this."

We'll play the part and give the bastard enough rope to hang himself. Harvey drew a breath, remembered Nat peering out the upper window with flames licking at her back. Anger surged through him, and he twisted it with false grief, ready to rail against Nat's supposed death.

"Ready," he said and pushed the doorbell.

Chimes rang through the house.

They waited.

Brayburn pushed the bell button.

A voice sounded inside. "I'm coming."

The deadbolt clicked open.

The door pulled back.

Curwood stood there.

"Andy, come on in. Conrad." He nodded at them. "This is a terrible event. I'm so sorry for your loss."

"Noted," Brayburn said. "Sorry to bother you, but since you've been in the Cove and in touch with folks there, we wanted to talk to you. Maybe you can help us piece together what's happened."

Curwood, clothed in a smoking jacket, led them into what appeared to be his den.

Pretentious fool. I don't think he even smokes. Harvey scanned the floor-to-ceiling bookshelves. *Leather covers. Impressive. Wonder if he reads them?*

Curwood gestured to overstuffed leather armchairs. "Have a seat. I'm happy to help. Constable Parker's death shocked me. Such a waste." He chose a chair with its back to the door.

Just where we want him. All the better for our surprise.

"Who called you?" Brayburn asked.

"I think it was a volunteer fireman," Curwood said. "Jones maybe? I didn't really catch it."

Probably because no one did call you. We've checked. You made a mistake thinking we'd take your word for it.

Harvey crossed his legs and gripped the chair arms. If he didn't, he'd jump up and punch the smugness out of the man. "And why did he call you?"

"Not really sure, although I've had dealings with the firefighters there from time to time. And people did know I'd been helping Parker with a few things. Probably didn't want me to hear it on the news." His sad face looked back at Harvey.

And Harvey's urge to punch the man escalated. *Smooth-talking liar. How many things over the years have you lied about?*

"Makes sense, I suppose." Brayburn relaxed in the chair, hands on the arms. "What's your assessment of what might have happened? After all, Parker and Conrad here were no longer on the case. Having an enforced vacation so to speak."

"Certainly true," Curwood said. "But Parker didn't leave it alone. She cooked up some nonsense about looking for the dead girl's friend. Amara Krause wasn't it?" He sighed. "Maybe she got too close to the person who killed those girls." He turned one hand toward Brayburn. "After all, you and I did discuss the risk in sending her out so soon after that explosion. Maybe she slipped up and gave herself away."

"Another possible theory. I'm sure the investigation will sort it all out."

A small noise in the hall caught Harvey's attention, and he cocked his head. The other men didn't seem to hear. *Nat and Turner are in the building.* He coughed. "Sorry, still have effects from the smoke."

Brayburn, alerted by Harvey's code phrase, sat forward, his arms resting on his thighs. "It's always hard to lose one of our own," he said and looked at the floor.

For a few moments, they maintained silence. Curwood ended the pause. "Do you have any idea who might have done this?"

"Actually," Brayburn said and looked up, a huge smile on his face. "We do and we even have a warrant to arrest him."

Curwood sat upright. "So soon? How did you find him?"

"It is as you say," Harvey added. "Constable Parker got close to the truth, and actually uncovered it. It's what led to her being left unconscious in the burning house."

Curwood's eyes narrowed. "How did you discover that?"

"The best way possible," Harvey said. "From a reliable witness." He levered to his feet and loomed over Curwood.

Curwood's disparaging laugh preceded his so-sure-of-himself words. "What? At that time of night? Out in the country. No one could have seen anything."

Brayburn stood, shifted and joined Harvey. Both looked over Curwood's head toward the door.

Nat stepped in, and Harvey winked at her. "Even in the dark, if you know the person you're looking at, it's easy to identify him," she said, "And even better when you can record the conversation."

Curwood launched out of his chair and whirled. His face drained a pasty white. His eyes went wide with shock.

"Rey, old friend, you look like you've seen a ghost." Brayburn pulled the warrant from his pocket. "Have a look, it's all in order and all the evidence is with the judge." He opened his phone and called the men in the car. "You're on. Bring the search warrant and go to work."

"Play it, Nat," Harvey said and took out the handcuffs. He hauled Curwood's hands back none too gently. "That's for Parker. Not too tight, I hope." He pushed Curwood forward until the man stood in front of Nat. "She's no longer on suspension, is she?" He asked Brayburn.

"Not at all."

Harvey smiled at Nat. "You want to do the formalities?"

"Damned straight I do," she said and began the routine caution. "Rey Curwood, you are under arrest for the murders of Gloria Roberts and Amara Krause on the night of August fifteenth and sixteenth, 1969 in the Hamlet of Caleb Cove, and for the attempted murder of a police officer, Constable Natalie Ann Parker, in Caleb Cove, last night." She used the official name for the Cove, just in case it was ever questioned.

EPILOGUE

As expected the murder charges against Rey Jarvis Curwood roared through the province. The investigation and charging dragged through every phase. Once it came to trial, the big shot lawyer Curwood had hired questioned and twisted all the evidence. Public opinion shifted every other week. And Curwood steadfastly denied the charges.

Constables Parker and Conrad came under attack, their lives scrutinized back to their births. Caleb's Cove became their safe haven. Devon and Greg returned to locking the gates on the estate, and Adam insisted Mutt stay with Natalie at all times. Other residents learned to identify reporters at a glance and send out the alert.

Gloria Roberts and Amara Krause's families received special permission to bury the girls, side-by-side, in the Caleb's Cove graveyard. They tracked the unfortunate girl originally buried in Gloria's place, to a family in Manitoba. She'd come east in August and never returned. In the end, three families received closure on the deaths of loved ones.

Matt Mackenzie, sober for the first time in years, stuck to his story and the documentation, including the recovery of the coat buttons with damning bloodstains, backed up his statement. He pleaded guilty to his part in the murder cover-up, negating any charges by Curwood's lawyer that he'd told his tale for leniency for himself. Early in the year, he'd been sentenced to serve fifteen years in prison.

Eighteen months after Curwood's arrest, the jury filed out for the final discussions. Deliberations lasted three days and then the word came down they were ready to return and deliver their final verdict.

Harvey returned to the gallery with Nat to hear the verdict. The whole row, and the ones behind and in front of them, were filled with the folk from Caleb's Cove. Doris Roberts and Lenya Krause sat on either side of Evelyn Gerber, their hands joined. They'd closed the stores, the café, the marina and the museum. Lem refused any tour bookings. The only one missing was Mutt.

All persons in the courtroom stood as the judge took his place. The jurors filed in, their eyes fixed steadily downward. Creaking seats, rustling clothing, and one large sneeze punctuated the hush in the room. "Sorry," Adam whispered to Natalie.

The court clerk faced the jury. "Would the foreman please stand."

The older man serving as foreman obeyed the directive.

"Have you reached a verdict?" asked the judge.

"Yes, sir, we have."

"What say you in the case of the attempted murder of Natalie Ann Parker by Rey Jarvis Curwood?"

"Guilty as charged."

Noise erupted through the room, and the judge banged his gavel. "Silence. Silence in the court."

"And in the case of the murders of Gloria Roberts and Amara Krause by Rey Jarvis Curwood?"

The foreman cleared his throat.

The room held its breath.

"Guilty as charged."

Chaos erupted, with so much noise, so much backslapping and so many hugs it took the judge a good five minutes to quiet the room.

"Rey Jarvis Curwood, you have been found guilty of all charges. Sentencing will be in two weeks. Please escort the prisoner to the cells." And he slammed his gavel once.

The Caleb's Cove residents filed out of the court and headed for the restaurant they'd booked in advance, certain of what the verdict would be. A buffet meal waited for them but eating did not halt the talk and laughter. In time, stuffed with food topped with a glass of wine here and there, the group calmed down.

Turner, usually the most silent one in the crew, rose and knocked on the table for attention. "There are folks who want to offer toasts."

Brayburn, who'd been invited to attend, stood. "First, here's to outstanding police work."

"Hear, hear." The agreeable response circled the room and glass were clinked and drinks were drunk.

Lem took over. "Second, here's to justice, as well as the law, being served properly."

"Absolutely," shouted Mrs. Gerber. "And thanks to you all."

Greg Cunningham and Devon stood together. "Third, here's to Natalie's new job with the Caleb Cove Security Agency," said Devon.

"We're looking forward to working with her," Greg added.

"Oh boy," shouted Adam, jumping up on his chair. "Mutt's gonna love that."

"And fourth," Turner actually grinned when he stood once again. "I've done some investigating on another matter. There are people in here who have been keeping a secret for a very long time. Please stand and toast the talented, loveable, and," he paused and grinned even wider, "MARRIED duo of Natalie Parker and Harvey Conrad."

Dead silence settled in the room for long minutes. The hurricane of noise that broke loose after caused people on the street to stop and look. Even Mutt, waiting back in Caleb's Cove probably heard the cheers.

Urged on by the clanking of dozens of spoons against as many glasses, Harvey stood, took Nat's hand and helped her to her feet. His kiss, solid, long and passionate, satisfied not only his wife, but the entire Caleb's Cove crew.

Harvey ended the kiss and turning Nat around, hugged her against him. "And now," he whispered, "everyone knows I have your back."

Blushing, Natalie smiled and accepted good wishes. Harvey had been right all along. Going back to work had been the best, well, the second best thing, she could do. At the moment, she had everything a person could want. Including Harvey.

About the Author- Mahrie G. Reid

Write what you want to read.

An avid reader from elementary school on, Mahrie often read twelve books a week. Once she'd read the Nancy Drew books, mysteries dominated her lists. Agatha Christie, Dick Frances and Dorothy Gilman, among many others, set the tone for her reading and writing.

Over the years she's published articles, poems and short stories. She has belonged to writing groups and attended conferences and workshops and, in later years, taught in all these areas. Her stories involve ordinary people who get caught up in extraordinary situations that push them to be more, and do more, than they ever thought possible.

Mahrie is a member of Alberta Romance Writers' Association and a graduate of Calgary's Citizen's Police Academy and Private Investigation 101. She lives north of Calgary, Alberta with her hubby and a cat called Kotah.

www.mahriegreid.com

www.facebook.com/mahriegreid

Other books by Mahrie

Caleb Cove Mysteries, Book 1

Came Home Dead

Be careful what you do in life for your past may come back to haunt *you.*

When a corpse surfaces in the aftermath of a hurricane, the storm has only begun for Devon Ritcey. Friends and family in Caleb's Cove offer up an excess of secrets and suspects. And her big secret can make her a suspect. Can she work with ex-cop, ex-lover, Greg Cunningham to uncover the killer and keep the island's inhabitants safe while guarding her own secrets?

Caleb Cove Mysteries, Book 2

Came Home to a Killing

All of our lives may be an illusion.

When Kelsey Maxwell learns her life is lie, she's determined to uncover the truth. She doesn't expect her quest to lead to fraud, murder, and a killer with a knife. Working with Sam Logan, a security consultant, she follows her father's trail chased by criminals who want evidence he's stolen. Caught in a race for the prize, Kelsey doesn't know if the truth will set her free, or get them all killed.

Caleb Cove Mysteries, Book 3

Came Home too Late

When revenge explodes into violence, both the guilty and the innocent can be caught in the fallout. Growing up on-the-run with her criminal father, Emily Martin knows only two truths; her safety depends on hiding in plain sight, and that the police are not her friends. But when the sins of her father's past catch up with her present, who in Caleb's Cove can she trust to help her fight for her life. In a race for the truth, will trust be the obstacle that destroys them all?

Made in the USA
Columbia, SC
24 February 2018